PRAISE

"Brooke Dean is an amazing author whose characters leap off the pages. Her imagination is off the chain and the writing is out of the box. A lot of people claim to write erotica, but this is authentic and will have many wanting to test the waters of the BDSM lifestyle by the time they finish reading."
~ ZANE, NYT BESTSELLING AUTHOR, PUBLISHER, DIRECTOR, AND PRODUCER

"[Brooklyn Unleashed] turned me on and as the Queen of Erotic, that is truly saying something.!"
~ ZANE, NYT BESTSELLING AUTHOR, PUBLISHER, DIRECTOR, AND PRODUCER

"In the climactic finale to the *Brooklyn Unbound* Trilogy - a tumultuous love triangle blending drama, passion, and betrayal that refuses to let go - Brooke Dean has masterfully balanced the elements of spice and story, delivering a perfect concoction that satisfies both the craving for steamy encounters and a narrative that is just as addicting. The palpable tension and seductive diversions orchestrated create a dangerous obsession, pushing the boundaries of love and loyalty. With an ending that defies predictions and leaves readers hungry for more, *Brooklyn Unraveled* solidifies Brooke Dean's place as not only a captivating storyteller, but a new favorite auto-buy author in the erotic romance genre."
~ PATTY K. RIVERA, OPS CONTENT SPECIALIST, AUDIBLE, INC.

Brooklyn Unraveled

A NOVEL

Written by Brooke Dean
Published by Brooke D. Dean
www.brookeddean.com

Distributed by IngramSpark

First printing. February 14, 2024.
ISBN: 978-1-962870-18-4

Dedication

For Jaxon: I love you, I love you, I love you! I also hope you are reading this dedication as an adult! You are the reason I do anything in this world and I'm so proud to be your mom.

Acknowledgments

To my family, friends and colleagues who have supported me – THANK YOU! Those people include:

Jaxon Dean McMillon, Donna L. Dean, Bruce H. Dean, Nicole D. Dahmani, Fouad Dahmani, Kyce A. Dahmani, Ibrahim A. Dahmani, Nadia A. Dahmani, Vivian Monserrate Cotte, Patty K. Rivera, Siniya Weldon, Nicole Ransome, Nicole Op Den Bosch, Phara Joseph, Margaret Hargrove, Yvonne Durant, my colleagues at Audible, Inc., Serena Wills, Julia Proctor, the Caviness family, and all of my sister friends who are too many to name. Time, space and modesty compel me to stop here, but I am truly blessed.

Lastly, to my dear readers - those who picked up, bought and/or shared any of my books - thank you for giving my words a chance. If you have found a tiny piece of yourself within these chapters, then my job is done. Your support means more than you could ever know and I hope you continue on this journey with me!

Brooklyn UNRAVELED

A NOVEL

BROOKE DEAN

One

It's barely light outside, but already there is so much about this morning that feels like I've woken up in some strange, alternate universe.

I'm in my apartment, of course. My family photos are on the walls in neat little frames, my favorite cherry ice cream is in the freezer. I'm in my kitchen, cracking some very normal-looking organic eggs from my neighborhood farmers' market into a basic glass bowl to get scrambled. All pretty regular stuff.

What I can't get over, however, is the presence of two extremely important people in my life – in said kitchen, with me. *At the same time.*

More than once, I've found myself staring, astounded into motion-lessness as I try to absorb what's happening around me in real life.

The tap-tap-tapping of J chopping onions on the island cutting board for the potatoes he's throwing into a skillet sizzling with melted butter.

My undergrad little sister, Bianca, humming along to some old school R&B playing on the kitchen speaker as she delicately pulls strips of turkey bacon out of the package, nestling them side by side in the pan she's set next to J's potatoes on the stove.

J's soft laugh as he tells her it'll be so much better if she roasts the bacon in the oven on high heat. Bianca's answering chuckle and claim that there's nothing on earth that can save turkey bacon in the first place.

As I gape at them in wonder, the corners of Bianca's mouth pull down briefly in an impressed expression before she turns away to dump the empty bacon package in the trash bin at the end of the island. "How do you know about that kind of stuff, anyway?" Bianca has never had any qualms about being nosy. I notice she's decided to take J's cooking advice when she slides a bacon-laden jellyroll pan into the oven – and makes me cringe when she lets the door slam, damn it.

I look to J, anticipating his answer a little more than I would ever admit aloud. The man I've known up to this moment would say something mysterious and aloof and effortless. Always revealing little more than nothing. Always leaving me wanting.

"My grandmother taught me," J says instead, "whenever I used to visit her in Jamaica in the summertime." He answers my sister with a simple, honest warmth and nostalgic little twinkle in his eye that instantly burns me up with jealousy. He's never told me anything like that, no matter how many different ways I've asked about his past.

There's a part of me – a rather large part, if I'm being honest – that wants to cross my arms and pout about how free J is being with information about himself with a family member of mine he barely knows, but… whatever. I'm much too mature to hate on my own sibling for too long, after all, so I ignore the prickly irritation making my hair stand on end and get back to my eggs.

It smells like a greasy spoon diner in here now, but instead of my being steeped in warm and fuzzy feelings like a normal person preparing breakfast with the people they love, anxiety has my shoulders bunched up around my ears.

Honestly, this family sitcom scenario playing out right now is that *last* thing I ever expected to happen. When I met J – especially considering the *way* we met – I had absolutely no intention of developing a long-term relationship, let alone introducing him to the family. I just wanted a chance to find out if I could meet a non-creepy guy who was into and willing to explore the same kinky things I was just discovering. How in the hell is he so chill and comfortable with my sister? And vice versa?

Bianca has only met a couple of guys I dated in the past and she wasn't keen on any of them. This morning feels so natural, even though the three of us have never been in the same room together before last night.

I should be thrilled, I know.

So why is it freaking me the fuck out?

Finally pouring the eggs into the hot pan, I scoot them around with my silicone spatula and will my racing heart to calm down. It makes no sense, but I feel so…untethered. Not necessarily *out* of control, but certainly not feeling like I *have* any at the moment. J just happened to pop up at my house while I was taking care of Bianca, and Lord knows I wouldn't have invited him over at that particular time with everything that was going on. Then Bianca basically walked over and forced her way into an introduction I wasn't prepared to make.

Sweat trickles down the small of my back that has nothing to do with the heat from the oven and I feel just the way I did a few hours ago when J arrived: like I've just grabbed onto the back of a speeding train and it's nearly ripped my arm out of the socket as it zooms down the track to parts unknown.

Both of them being here is so nice. *Amazing,* even. And the two of them seem to be getting along great, but…this isn't the way I'd planned to integrate these two very different parts of my life.

Fine, maybe I didn't have a solid plan in place yet, but that isn't the point.

I wasn't ready for this. Not yet.

I was still trying to figure out exactly what J and I were doing.

Hell, I still am.

"So, you know you're gonna tell me how y'all *really* met, right?"

My sister's annoyed drawl pulls me out of my daze.

Blinking as I reemerge from my thoughts, I turn and face Bianca, who's standing at my hip with her arms crossed. She gives me the same stare our mother uses when she knows we're lying about something and is waiting for us to tell the truth so she can dole out punishment. Honestly, it's beyond disturbing to see such an uncanny imitation of my mother's expression on such a young face. Bianca probably doesn't even know she's doing it.

I look past her into the kitchen and find the island noticeably empty. "Where'd J go?"

"He said to the bathroom, but you're not getting out of this."

I roll my eyes and get back to babysitting my breakfast contribution even as my stomach does a nervous, nauseous flip. The eggs in my pan are getting less and less appealing. I really don't want to eat anything right now. "Get out of what? I don't know you're talking about."

I know exactly what she's talking about.

"*Please.*" I can feel Bianca's eyes narrow – again, just the way our mothers would – without even looking at her. "I thought I'd be nice and not force you to spill all the details while the man was still standing at your front door," she says, "but trust and believe I wanna hear everything *right now*. I saw how panicked you looked when you introduced him, but I think you've had enough time to adjust."

"Excuse me?" I force a laugh I don't feel and a smile I have no doubt she doesn't believe, but I can't help it. My brain needs time to rally so I can defend myself here.

"Did you meet him in an alley or something?" My sister's surprised chuckle sounds genuine. "Why are you being so weird?"

"*No,* Bianca, I did not meet him in an alley. Jesus." I've been so distracted my cooked eggs are just shy of rubbery. I scoop a small pile onto the three plates she's placed on the counter next to the stove. She falls into step behind me, arranging bacon slices artfully next to the steaming eggs.

"So," Bianca continues, her voice lowering as she glances over her shoulder to make sure the coast is clear, "how did you meet him for real?"

Okay, what options do I have here? I could tell my kid sister the truth – that I met J on an app geared toward folks many would consider to be sexual deviants…and we kind of stumbled into a real-life relationship that was *supposed* to solely be about fucking in the most creative ways possible – but what kind of message would that send to her? I'm super grown and I'm only just now coming around to accept my sexual proclivities; I don't know if I'm ready to expose them to my family yet. Especially my younger sister who, in my mind, is still impressionable.

I could always lie, but then Bianca has always had a knack for sniffing out the bullshit in people around her. I learned that long ago. And honestly, I don't know if I want to be counted among those in her life, she's unable to fully trust, even if this is a situation that's relatively trivial.

If you want to be better, you have to *do* better.

Maybe I can tell her most of the truth?

"We met on an app."

"Okay…what kind of app?"

I grit my teeth. "A *dating* app, Bianca."

She pauses, her lips pursing as she leans closer to peer into my face. "What *kind* of dating app?"

"For singles, Bianca – damn!"

She throws her head back and laughs, absolutely delighted by my discomfort. I just want to put both hands around her neck and squeeze – just a little bit – but I manage to resist.

"Fine," she says, still chuckling, and finally lets it drop.

For all of two seconds, I feel like I can breathe.

Then Bianca's playful smirk takes on a devilish edge and I know I'm in trouble.

"Did you swipe right on him just to take a ride on that dick?"

"*BIANCA!*" I swear black spots invade my vision – I might actually pass out. I have never heard her talk this way – what the hell happened to my baby sister?

I can't even get my mouth to cooperate. "What – I – *who are you right now?*"

Bianca just cackles again and I can't understand why she's enjoying this so much.

"I had no idea you were such a prude, sis. I bet you probably think I'm still a virgin." She clucks her tongue at me with a disapproving shake of her head, sending her long braids bouncing.

I did think exactly that – or at least *hoped* Bianca hadn't already dived headfirst into the turbulent waters of sex and romance, but I have no intention of telling her that. Besides, my bugged-out eyes and gaping mouth are probably enough confirmation of my thoughts all on their own.

Looking past her at the hallway, I find J is still conspicuously absent. Only way he's still in the bathroom at this point is if he's taking a gigantic dump, which I highly doubt based on what I know about his meticulous hygiene habits. I don't even think he's passed gas in the same room as me at his own place, let alone drop a deuce in *my* apartment with my family present. No way his disappearing act isn't intentional.

This time, I'm the one shaking my head. He saw my dread when I tore out of the club last night, my relief when he found me at home afterward and she was here as well. But if he witnessed those things, J must also have seen the concern about her still weighing me down like a lead jacket.

I see what he's doing and he's right; I need to have a real, substantive talk with my sister. The fact that I have literally no details regarding Bianca reaching such a huge milestone of womanhood has left me more than a little shook. I'm her big sister and should have known something like that when it happened, not potentially years after the fact.

But another time. Right now, she wants to know about *my* life, and I need to be open and let her if I want to do better than I have been with our relationship.

I top our plates with some paper towels and truly face her, looking at her eye to eye. "There was no swiping left or right, okay? He saw my profile and my *non-naked* pics and messaged me. We hit it off right away."

Crossing her arms, Bianca gave me an appraising stare. "Okay, and then what?"

Better to give her the abridged version that didn't include all the wild, freaky sex. "We talked on the phone until we felt comfortable enough to meet up in person – which we did in a very public place. I liked him and he liked me, and we've been hanging out ever since."

"Hm." She casts a pensive glance at where J had disappeared, as if trying to see the shape of the man in the empty space between the wall sconces. Then she shrugs. "Well, dude is extremely fine – can't lie about that. And he seems to be a fairly decent human being, honestly." She turns a sudden grin on me and I feel my eyes getting misty. "I guess you didn't do too bad," she says.

"Thanks," I say, the emotional rollercoaster ride from panic to shock to abject relief leaving me lightheaded. "But look – I got lucky, okay? *You* need to leave all those dating apps alone, little girl." I wag my finger in her face for emphasis.

"Oh my *God,*" Bianca says, her face twisting up as she gently swats my hand away. "I haven't been a 'little girl' in years, Brooklyn."

"Try a couple of days ago," I say with a snort, partly to cover up the sudden sinking feeling in my gut because I realize it's only half a joke even as I say it. Sometimes it really does feel like I blinked and she was a fully-formed, fully-functional adult.

Well, maybe semi-functional, but still…not so long ago I would have to hold her little hand whenever we needed to cross the street.

Bianca must have seen traces of that bittersweet wistfulness in my eyes. The smug grin that had revealed her dimples fades, melting into something tender and almost sad.

My throat tightens and clogs with the jumble of all the things suddenly I want to say with a fierceness that leaves me blinking back real tears out of nowhere. It's like I can see all the little moments I wasn't around her since I was grown and out of the house stretching out before me now in a solid chain, adding up to years of time I can never get back. And years may as well be decades when it comes to growing up.

How did I let that happen without my having truly been involved?

I feel like I missed it.

My mouth drops open to speak – to say what, I have no idea – but J strolls back into the kitchen with a sly grin of his own and my mouth snaps shut just as quickly.

"Hope I'm not interrupting anything," he says, his carefully curated words as smooth as his gait back to the kitchen island.

I cut my eyes at him when he throws me a wink but I know my look doesn't have the sharp edge I meant it to. He knows good and well he's just walked in on a *moment* – one I know has already faded away as Bianca's attention flutters back to J. But I understand why he created the space for it. It just wasn't enough.

There's so much I want to say I don't know what to do with it all, but I can't have a feminine heart-to-heart with Bianca with J here, his intensely masculine vibe sucking up all the energy in the room.

Squealing in alarm when she realizes the potatoes are sticking to the pan, Bianca dashes back to the stove and starts feverishly pushing them around with a wooden spoon she snatches out of the holder on the counter.

J laughs as he pulls three glasses out of the cupboard, gathering all three in his huge hands with little effort. "I thought you knew what you were doing over there."

I spin on him then. "Uh, weren't you supposed to be setting the table – over there?" I jerk my thumb in the direction of the living room.

Bianca giggles and gives a quick snap of her fingers with her free hand, still stirring with the other. "*That* part, sis."

Smiling, I shake my head. Though I appreciate the endorsement, the potatoes are probably a lost cause at this point. But I know my sister has no plans on giving up; it's just not in her nature.

"I see sass runs in the family," J says, and Bianca stops plating the half-burnt hash and slams the pan onto the counter, sending a few oily spuds flying across the granite surface and onto the floor.

She whirls on J, hand on her hip. "You're goddamn right – and where are you going without the napkins, anyway? Can you get them and set the table like you have some sense? We are not savages."

Across the room, J tenses. My eyes dart back and forth between my sister and my boyfriend like I'm waiting for one of them to move a muscle and set off a land mine. The fuck? Why the hell is Bianca talking to J like that? I thought they were getting along.

They both burst out laughing and I stumble back a step-in shock. Somehow, in the hours since I introduced them, Bianca and J have developed *this* level of rapport with each other? I don't even know what to do with that.

So, I don't do anything but try to let myself enjoy it from there, to stop fighting what is so clearly a good thing. By the time we're all sitting around the table and stuffing our faces, I've managed to get my shoulders to relax and laugh along at their good-natured needling of each other, adding my own jabs here and there.

Bianca is relating some wild story about one of her professors going in on a sleeping student when J pulls my bare foot up into his lap and begins gently kneading my instep with his thumb under the table as she speaks, gesturing wildly with her hands.

It's an intimate yet harmless gesture and one he's done countless times. But when his fingers inadvertently stroke my ankle, it reminds me of something Nikki did the last time we were together. Which makes me think of her wild-ass, bizarre "gift".

Just like that, all the tension in my body returns with a vengeance.

Why would she send me something like that?

No matter how many times I try to stay present, even as Bianca's rapid-fire questions to J reveal anecdotes from his past I've never heard before, I can't enjoy it. I keep thinking about Nikki's panties and what they could mean.

J gallantly offers to clean up the breakfast dishes once we're done eating and I indulge Bianca in putting on some old movie she wants to see while he finishes up.

She slides me a knowing glance as I set up the movie on the living room TV and settle onto the couch. "Keep him," she mouths to me as she sits on the floor and crosses her legs, making me smile to myself. If only she knew how much she looks like a little kid right now…

We end up doing this the rest of the day. J never mentions his need to be anywhere else, and neither does Bianca. After the second movie, J orders delivery and we munch on gigantic sandwiches and fries until J and my sister pass out where they sit in a carb coma.

I'm not so lucky. I want to go to sleep right along with them so badly, but all I can think about is Nikki's panties in that stupid box. Just bizarre on top of weird.

What did she mean by "without you-know-who"? I know she was referring to J, but was she saying she wanted a relationship with just me alone? Was she just talking about sex? Or something else altogether?

God, I don't know and it's driving me nuts. And I can't get up and pace like I want to because J has conveniently fallen asleep on top of my feet.

I want to revel in his comfy weight and warmth, but I can't with these questions burning through my brain.

Dirty panties, though? Really, Nikki? The twisted parts of myself that think that's beyond hot must be too drowsy to care, because right now, it's just gross and disturbing.

I should get rid of them.

I don't know why the thought of actually doing it brings me pause.

Jesus, do I actually *want* to keep them? What does that say about me?

And I still need to tell J about it. So strange that he hasn't asked.

When I look up, I find warm eyes staring back at me and I swear he read my thoughts. His mouth opens in a wide yawn but I know his mind is awake and sharp when he says, "You never did tell me who sent you a gift, Gorgeous." J's voice rumbles, extra deep and rough from hours of disuse. "What was in that box I gave you?"

Two

My first instinct is to childishly pretend like I didn't hear J's question, so I cock my head at him and gesture at the TV, as if the volume is up too high. Which I know he doesn't buy, especially since Bianca is knocked out asleep in a ball on the floor.

It's also highly likely that my sister could sleep soundly through a nuclear bomb, but J doesn't know that.

I may not know what I want to do about the contents of that box, or the person who left it on my doorstep, but I *do* know I don't want to talk about it right now. Not with J, not with myself.

J gave me some emotional privacy and didn't ask about the box when he gave it to me or in the hours afterward, presumably because he was waiting for me to offer up the info without any prompting. But I haven't, and I've known him long enough now to understand that once he puts the question out there, he expects some kind of answer sooner rather than later.

Just thinking about that box – about Nikki herself – brews up a storm of emotions that buffets me from the inside out and makes me close my eyes for a moment. I don't want to deal with it. I don't want to discuss it. But I know what to do.

It takes a conscious effort to shove thoughts of my assistant to the corner of my mind, but once I do just that and open my eyes again, I make my intentions known to J in as seductive a whisper as I can manage.

"The only box I'm worried about right now is mine."

Maybe not the sexiest thing I've ever said, but J's answering eyebrow raise and eye flick to my sleeping sister's form tells me he's picking up what I'm putting down. If I give him bedroom eyes long enough, his massive dick will make its presence known for sure.

But I don't feel like waiting. I'm tired of *Nikki this, Nikki that* bouncing around in my mind, driving me nuts. J's hands haven't touched my body in what feels like days, even if it was technically only a few hours ago.

Right now, I need him. Only him.

I don't say anything else. J sits up just enough to allow me to push my body up off the couch. I jerk my head at the hallway parallel to the kitchen and pad silently to my bedroom, knowing he'll follow.

The heat of his big body warms me from behind before I can cross the threshold. He doesn't let me deal with the door myself, grabbing the steel handle and easing it shut so the only sound I hear is the lock engage with a subtle click.

With the lights still off, all I can see are shades of shadow as my eyes adjust to the dark, but all my other senses light up and fire in the vacuum left by my lack of sight.

After pressing my back against the door, J's nose grazes my jawline up to my ear. His pelvis presses hard into mine, making my breath hitch as need spikes hard and fierce inside me, spearing me through the core.

His neck is close enough to lick and I close my eyes since my vision is useless at the moment. J doesn't smell like the sweetness of vanilla and jasmine like Nikki. He's all spring sunshine and cool breezes blowing through sturdy oak trees — earthy and warm, with a hint of something leathery and wild and possibly dangerous. Not a manufactured scent in a bottle, either. Just his skin.

I love it as much now as I did when we met.

"You want me to turn on a light?" Hearing the hoarseness of my own voice in my ears doesn't make me cringe with embarrassment anymore.

It's just the intensity between J and I having its way, and he's taught me to trust it and let go.

"No need." J's soft lips brush against my earlobe as he whispers, making me shiver nicely. I know where he's going with this. He's using my entire bedroom as a blindfold.

I answer with a moan when he kisses me hard then whimper in frustration when he pulls away just as suddenly. "You have to promise to be quiet for me," J says. A slow thumb strokes over my cheekbone, my parted lips. "We have a guest and don't want to be rude."

My entire body thrums under his touch. Oh, I love it when I have to be quiet and know I can't – the fact that I have to suppress everything I'm feeling heightens the pleasure to the point of near-pain.

I'm already panting.

Right now, this is J's world and I'm just living in it.

His hand slides up my side, slow and deliberate so I can feel every finger pressing into my skin before he grabs ahold of a breast beneath my shirt. Tweaks my nipple. Rolls it between thumb and forefinger.

He's done little more than reach second base and I'm already climbing the walls, writhing with the effort it's taking to keep from mewling like a cat in heat. My panties are soaked.

Probably like that pair Nikki sent me.

Goddammit. I blink into the darkness; grateful J is distracted with leaving a trail of wet kisses along my collarbone and has no chance of catching the panicked expression I know my face is wearing right now.

This moment is not about Nikki. I'm not thinking about her or those sticky fucking panties.

I'm not.

J's hand closes gently around my throat and I'm immediately back in the game.

"You with me?" J licks at my lips, nibbles on my chin.

"Definitely," I say.

Which is apparently all the permission he needs to act on whatever's on his mind. That hand at my throat squeezes a little more firmly and he plants a solid kiss square on my mouth. "Turn around, Gorgeous."

Even if my mind had wanted to resist, my aching pussy would have paid it no mind. My body turns in his hold like it had been born to do it, my entire being begging for what it knows is coming.

J's hands hover at the band of my pajama bottoms on either side of my hips for a moment before yanking them along with my panties down to the floor. I help out and kick the pile of fabric out of our way, leaving my bare legs in a wide stance. I've been in this particular position with J enough times now to know exactly what to do.

I almost yelp when the palm of his hand lands firmly between my legs, stilling against the wet lips there for a moment before sliding up and back, deep into the crack of my ass. Two of his fingers circle and probe at my entrance. I'm so keyed up; the feeling makes my insides twist up with the ferocity of my need.

"I'm taking this ass tonight and you're gonna be quiet as a mouse. Right, Gorgeous?"

I nod like a good girl and wriggle my backside against the crotch of his pants.

J's fingers tighten around my throat just enough to be uncomfortable, triggering another rush of wetness between my open thighs.

"I didn't hear you answer," he purrs, his words hot against my neck.

"I—I'll be quiet," I say, whispering for emphasis that I heard his clear command, but my level of control comes into question when what feels like a very wet thumb begins working itself into my asshole.

It's all I can do to trap the moans in my throat, pleasure mingling with the discomfort until the former is all I feel, like a billion little snaps of electricity under my skin promising to set me ablaze.

My heart jumps when I hear J's zipper. The familiar weight of his smooth thickness tapping each of my ass cheeks in preparation has me licking my lips.

God – I can't wait, can't be still. I almost can't believe how much I want this.

I pray Bianca's still sleeping soundly as J begins to work himself inside, rocking against me, his hand creeping up from my throat to firmly cover my mouth.

Stretch, burn. Stretch, burn. Then pleasure so intense it makes my eyes roll back in my head. Already it feels like there's no more room in my body for him. I feel full to capacity, but J just keeps giving me more. And more.

There's always *more.*

My mouth drops open in a silent scream because we've only been at this for a few minutes and I've just about reached my limit. J, however, seems intent on pushing past them tonight and I'm just here for the ride.

"Can you feel me, Gorgeous?" I can hear the dark laughter in J's smoky voice even with his mouth pressed against the back of my nape.

My teeth gnash at his palm in answer. My legs are trembling so hard, J's supportive arm around my middle is the only thing holding me upright.

J chuckles, then grunts when he pulls out slowly to push right back in, making me arch my back and clench my teeth to keep from falling headfirst into a loud climax. "We're only halfway."

If this man keeps this up, I'm going to come so hard I won't be able to remember my own name, let alone Nikki's. At least for a little while.

And that's exactly what I want: orgasmic peace. No matter how temporary it will be.

My insides continue to give as J pushes forward incrementally and retreats again and again, drawing a silent and desperate gasp from me every time. My clit is so swollen it feels alive, throbbing in time with J's movements. I would barely have to touch it to go off like a bomb.

Without thinking, I reach down intending give myself a stroke or two, seeking my own bliss.

J grabs my hand as soon as it drops heavily against my thigh and wrenches it behind me, forcing my back into an even deeper arch. The sudden deeper angle of his entry makes me shoot up onto my tip toes with a gasp at the blinding pleasure. Maybe J could tell from the way my breathing changed or my spine straightened that I was teetering on the edge. Regardless of the how, he knows my body so well he understands how to save me from myself. His thrusts have picked up speed and the bass of his grunts have deepened, so I know he's not ready to be done yet.

Neither am I.

Stretching out my arms, I place my palms flat on the door just as J is pulling out to regroup. The shivers start up again when he runs appreciative fingers over the curve of one of my breasts and down the length of my spine.

I stick my ass out like an offering.

Take it.

At this point, I want to come so badly, I almost wouldn't care if my sister walked right on in. Almost.

J takes my open invitation and slides right back into my back door, pressing a hand over my mouth once more, but even more firmly this time, letting me make a little noise and still not be heard beyond the bedroom door.

Thank God, because I could not be silent anymore at this point if my life depended on it. J pumps and pants and I growl right into the palm of his hand, the tension in my shoulders and back and trembling, aching legs poised to snap. Heat seethes through me, starting at my center to flow through my sprawled limbs and back again. I don't realize I'm sweating until my lashes clump with it. Or it could be tears; J is about to turn me inside out and it's so good, I feel like I'm dying.

No sooner do I start slamming my ass back against him to create some of the friction my pussy is craving than J's arm tightens around me and I feel myself being hauled toward the bed. He pushes lightly and I conveniently fall face-first onto the mattress, my feet still on the floor. I spread my legs the way I did before and J falls right back into position. This time, though, he holds my cheeks apart with both hands, gripping my hips to give himself better access.

He holds me hard enough to bruise, but I love it. I love the heat of his smooth brown skin against mine, the stiff brush of his pants hitting all my slick parts from behind with every thrust.

I never want him to stop, but I can tell he's close from the way he twitches inside me.

J leans over, covering my entire torso with his own as he speaks into my ear once again. "I'll let you tell me where you want this cum…do you want it inside?"

As tempting as that is, the logical part of my brain wakes up a bit and decides it doesn't want to deal with messy aftermath of that with my sister still in the house.

I shake my head, then remember J can still barely see me. "On me," I say, rolling my hips in a circle to tempt him. That's a hell of a lot easier in terms of clean-up.

J licks the back of my neck before standing upright again, then starts pounding away like he's trying to punish me. I snatch up a nearby pillow and practically smother myself with it, biting down on the fabric to quell the inevitable noise. But if I can hear my desperate squeaks, J can as well. He reaches around then and finally moves his hand over my aching pussy, and at that point, it's only a matter of moments before I'm pulsing and clenching and twisting on the bed. Seconds after that, J gasps and I feel his length pull out of me just before hot streams of his seed land across my lower back. A hum of contentment buzzes in my throat as some of it pools in the small of my back and drips down my hip. So primal…it's shockingly rare that he wants to do this and I find myself reveling in it.

With the final blissful pulses of my climax echoing faintly in my bones, I pull myself forward onto the bed until my arms and legs are stretched straight across my fluffy duvet. J sighs and settles down beside me. I feel him roll onto his back and I place my hand flat on his chest, just to feel his heat soak into my palm and the rapid rise and fall of his firm chest as he catches his breath.

Neither of us speak, but we don't have to when we're like this. If nothing else, J has always seemed to understand me in the bedroom better than I did myself. Once I'm in his arms, he knows when I want to be loud or quiet, when I want him to take control or let me pilot the ship. I may have been all woman when we met, but he was still the author more sexual firsts than I can count.

Right now, J is giving me space to parse through my own thoughts, and I'm allowing him the same courtesy. Which is all good, until thoughts of Nikki start pushing their way back to the forefront of my mind.

My dopey smile is already dimming. The session with J doesn't turn out to be the quick fix to my mental dilemma I had hoped for. Pretty telling of my emotional state if I'm not drowsy and blissed out post-nookie for at least an hour.

I'm wide awake, listening to J's breathing as it slows. The rapid thumps of his heartbeat against my hand have begun to normalize.

Now, all I can think about is the way his pulse raced when Nikki and I were fucking him together.

Did his heart beat faster that night because she was there?

Did mine?

What a chilling thought.

This time, I roll over until I'm staring up at the ceiling with J. I still can't see him very well, but I hazard a glance at his profile anyway. If I can't get Nikki off my mind, I imagine she's had to run through J's head a few times since the night of club.

My teeth find my bottom lip. I could just ask him, couldn't I? I *did* just declare him my boyfriend in front of my little sister. I should be able to talk to my significant other about his feelings on the public threesome we shared with my co-worker…

God, that sounds demented even in my own head.

My fingers pick at the duvet. J still hasn't spoken and I'm finding it more and more difficult to be still and lay there like there isn't fifty pounds of guilt weighing down my chest.

Maybe the night with Nikki wasn't a big deal to J at all and I'm blowing this way out of proportion. But still…he doesn't know about the panties yet. That could change his perception of things considerably.

I should tell him. He did ask, but then again, he hasn't brought it back up.

Could he have let it go already?

The pros and cons ping-pong their way through my head. Making a decision has never been this difficult for me. It's like meeting J — and subsequently, discovering the naughty side of my long-time work assistant – has somehow rewired the way I think. I became the TV producer I am today because I learned early on how to prioritize what I wanted in my life and be ruthless about cutting out anything that wasn't important. When it comes to my love life over the past few months, all of that is clear as mud.

If I tell J that Nikki gifted me a pair of her worn panties with a note that suggested she was interested in getting me alone and he doesn't want me to see her again…I'm not sure how I'd feel about that. I'm going to *have* to see her at work, for one thing. She's the best assistant I've ever had and we work well together; I wouldn't want to have to start from scratch with a new trainee. Besides, the last thing I need is a wrongful termination suit if things got too weird and I felt like I needed to fire her. So, Nikki stays in terms of work, no question.

But I know J wouldn't feel all that comfortable with my continuing to see Nikki at the club or anywhere else outside of the workplace without him.

I just don't want him to give me an ultimatum. Because I'm not sure if I would respond the way J hopes I would.

A frustrated breath puffs from my lips. Let me get up and get in the shower since laying here isn't getting my life together.

The moment I sit up and move to slide off the bed, J's raspy voice finally breaks the silence and I freeze.

"I think we should talk about the club."

By "the club" he absolutely means "Nikki". Once again, J manages to read my mind. This strange trait of his used to be pretty charming; right now, it's just distressing.

The bed dips and moves underneath me a second before the lamp on my nightstand turns on, making me squint from the onslaught of light. Great, now there's no hiding anything, not even my facial expressions.

Choosing my words with the utmost care to avoid giving away my apprehension, I say, "What about the club?" If I let J take the lead on this conversation, I'll have a chance at managing my responses like a sane adult instead of a jittery teenager.

Settling back into his spot beside me, J props himself up on an elbow. His eyes drift over my face for a second before he smirks and meets my gaze. "Oh, you don't know what I'm talking about? That's what we're doing?"

Of course, he knows I'm being avoidant.

And I have no plans to stop for the time being.

Since the lights are on and I can no keep my expressive face to myself, I lean into the exposure quite literally, stripping my pajama top over my head. When I toss it aside, I exaggerate the movement and arch my back so my breasts jiggle a little more than usual.

His eyes drop to my chest and a surge of victory pulses through me. "We have plenty of time to talk about a whole lot of things," I say, crawling backward off the bed. When I get to my feet, I reach forward to grab his hands and pull him up with me. "Right now, we both need a shower."

Relief makes me a little weak in the knees when J doesn't resist and follows me to the bathroom. When I glance back at him over my shoulder, however, he looks more resolute than I would like.

"Brooklyn." He tugs on my hand to get me to stop. That look on his face intensifies and I have to swallow the lump that lodges in my throat. "Be careful around Nikki. I know you've dealt with her at work for a long time now, but there's sides to her that you don't know about."

A frown settles between my brows. J seems so *sure* about that. He honestly thinks he knows my assistant better than I do overall?

I resist the urge to roll my eyes. "I might know more than you think I do. Besides, I'm a big girl, J. I can handle myself."

His mouth quirks up on one side. "That's not all you can handle."

So lame and not J's style at all – I can't help but burst out laughing. It's a welcome respite from the tension I've been feeling.

I yank him into the bathroom and lock the door. The entire room gets balmy with the steam from the shower in no time, and soon J has me pressed against the tile, a wet washcloth stuffed into my mouth to keep my cries from echoing off the slick walls.

Three

There's hardly anyone in the building when I show up to work the next day. That does nothing to stop my heart from jumping into my throat every time I tiptoe around a corner in my campaign to look as busy as possible.

I'm running my own errands this morning for the first time in forever – setting up the conference room for the morning meeting with coffee cups and fresh pastries supplied by the bakery on the ground floor of the building, organizing the stacks of papers on my desk so it at least looks like the person who works there knows what she's doing. Things my assistant would normally do. Back when my life actually made sense.

Getting the jump on Nikki turns out to be way more difficult than I had anticipated since she usually gets to work so damn early. It's been years since I've managed to beat her here, and the few times I have were only happenstance. Let it never be said that the woman is not a hard worker.

Only the morning cleaning crew and a couple of diehard assistant producers who don't have lives outside of work are here now, sharing the floor with me in their respective offices. The huge wall of windows on the east side of the building reveals a morning filled with gray clouds, barely tinted pink with the rising sun. Inside is so still and quiet, a fly buzzing down the main hallway would sound like a lawnmower.

Well, at least to me. Every time I hear the main elevator doors ding in the lobby at the front of the station's suite of offices, my stomach twists into a tighter knot. I can't remember the last time I was this nervous. My palms have been slick with sweat ever since I arrived on the subway. I couldn't even make myself stop to get my usual quick breakfast from my favorite bodega since I was way too keyed up to eat anything.

Unfortunately for me, Nikki has kept up with my monthly schedule so well that everything I need is set for the first part of the day in less than an hour. I have nothing to do but twiddle my thumbs until my first meeting. I can't make myself sit down at my desk for longer than a few seconds at a time, so I get up and pace the halls and empty conference rooms in my sneakers for a while, pumping my arms and pretending to be exercising for anyone around curious enough to wonder what the hell I'm doing.

I check my watch as I walk, chewing my lip. It's past six. From what's she's told me in the past, Nikki would have been here twenty or so minutes ago on a regular work day, and earlier than that if there was some special event in the office for which she had to help prepare.

I slept so little last night after J and Bianca finally went home, the caffeine flowing through my bloodstream from the espresso I've just thrown back is the only thing keeping me on my feet. All I've been able to think about are hypothetical conversations involving the same question I need to ask Nikki – why did you do it and what does it mean? Dozens of versions of the same scene have played out in my mind's eye and I haven't been satisfied with any of their conclusions. I want Nikki to remain in my professional life for sure. I also want her in my life outside of this office, but in what capacity, I'm still haven't been able to nail down. There're too many holes in the picture of Nikki beyond these walls, and lately, every interaction I've had with her just reveals more. I need answers in order to move forward. But I'd be lying if I said I'm not halfway afraid to know the whole truth.

To distract myself, I jump at the opportunity to make small talk with a member of the uniformed cleaning crew who's finishing up in the bathroom. He looks surprised I'm talking to him at all and halfway into our one-sided exchange, he gives me a benign smile and puts his earbuds back in with a quick wave, effectively ending our encounter.

So much for that. Having already run out of people to talk to, I keep wandering in circles, drifting in and out of offices I keep finding empty. I wave and grin brightly at the few producers and managers already on the job as I pass their open doorways. They wave back slowly, smiling back in confusion.

The elevator bell goes off just as my feet carry me to the main lobby. My heart drops into my stomach.

Just as quickly, I have to place a hand on my chest to calm my heart when a sense of relief hits my body like a linebacker in the Super Bowl. It's only Debbie Penn, my producer mentor and good friend. She's putting something in her huge designer bag and her green eyes go wide as saucers when she looks up to see me standing there.

"Brooklyn? I don't think I've ever seen you here this early." Shaking her head, she smirks and resumes her brisk pace toward her office, which is down the hall from mine.

I fall into step beside her with a chuckle, linking my elbow with hers. "Good morning to you, too."

"You must think I'm too old to make it to my office without an escort. For your information, these joints don't contain even a hint of the arthritis you think I have." Debbie's sharp eyes look me up and down as we walk. Her bobbed hair gleams under the fluorescent lights, the sharp angle brushing her jaw. "Do you have a cane hidden somewhere, too?"

I laugh. How is she so saucy this early in the day? I've always admired that about her. She takes shit from no one, not even me, her protégé. "You're way too sensitive about your age, Deb. It's a credit to your fabulousness that you're still the reigning queen around here."

"I've forgotten how much I enjoy your flattery, Brooklyn." Debbie chuckles as we arrive at her office, unlocking the door and walking inside to her desk. I hover at the doorway. It's been a good long while since I had a real chat with her and I'd like to catch up in a real way. I really have to do better about maintaining all the relationships in my life and not be so stuck in my own head.

I ask Deb about her family and she catches me up a little on the recent vacation she went on with her husband and grown kids. Physically, I'm present – I laugh and smile and nod at the appropriate times. Mentally, I'm somewhere else entirely. The threat of Nikki catching me unawares hovers over me like a dark cloud and I can't shake it. I need to talk to her but I want it to be on my own terms.

And I can only do that if she brings her ass to work – it's nearly seven now and she still hasn't stepped off that elevator.

"Hey, Deb," I say once she's paused long enough to log into her computer, one eye watching the empty hallway, "your schedule open enough to grab dinner later this week? It's been forever." The naked surprise in her expression when she looks up from her desk stings a little. I smile to hide the needle of guilt I feel in my chest. "Besides, I wanna hear all about the grandkids. I know you've been dying to tell anybody willing to listen."

The way Debbie's face lights up makes it worth braving the potential awkwardness of my impromptu invitation being turned down. "They *are* getting big," Debbie says, giggling. When she gets like this, it's easy to forget she's nearly twenty years older than I am. That and all the yoga she does in her office on her lunch breaks that keeps her far more limber than even the youngest folks that work for the station. "I love that idea. Just text me and we'll set something up. There's a new place a couple blocks over I've been dying to try."

My chest warms with affection. "Sounds good. Just let me know and I'll be there."

She waves and smiles up at me. "See ya, kid."

Well, Debbie *is* a busy woman. Having been dismissed in the kindest possible way, I wave back and make my way back to my own office. Time for me to get down to business.

My heart gives a nervous little flutter when I enter the space, my eyes darting around as if I'd find Nikki hiding behind my office chair. But there's no one, just me by myself looking crazy.

I spot the area on my desk where's I'd usually find my breakfast this time of morning, all neatly set out with the black coffee I always need to power through all the crap I have to do in a day. It's empty.

I go from being nervous about Nikki showing up to feeling worried that she might not come to work today at all.

She keeps a stock of granola bars in my desk for hunger-related emergencies, when nothing else can salvage my energy levels during a mid-afternoon slump. Fishing one out of its box in one of my drawers, I unwrap it and stuff the whole thing in my mouth.

It feels weird eating breakfast at work by myself. At home, it's pretty uncommon as J and I are usually together or I was so tired the night before I sleep right through until lunchtime. Nikki and I gossiping over some tasty grub she made herself or found at some neighborhood gem has been a daily ritual for years now.

Though I happen to really like this brand of granola bar, all I taste is sadness. I don't even have it in me to put on some music to buffer all the silence pressing in on my eardrums.

In a way, I miss her. I miss the normalcy of the two of us in here, planning our workday over a shared meal, laughing over her collection of dick pics from all the guys who've tried to get with her over the years.

I sigh, a sense of weariness settling over me. Things between Nikki and I used to be much less complicated.

Perhaps if I focus on the things in my life that seem to have worked themselves out, I'll feel better.

Last night with J was absolutely delicious; I was boneless after we did it again in the shower – the old-fashioned way the second time around. Eventually, I told him I was feeling conflicted about Nikki but that I'd heed his warnings about her. I still haven't told him about the panties and he hasn't asked about the box again. I guess knowing I'll listen to him was enough to satisfy J for now. I certainly hope so.

If Nikki hasn't shown up by now, she's not going to. I heard the receptionist come in while I was chatting with Deb; I'm willing to bet she'll have a note for me that Nikki called in sick when I make my way up there to get my mail.

The thought helps me relax for the first time since I arrived this morning. After taking a couple of deep breaths, I pull my cell out of my purse slung across the back of my chair and check my messages.

Nothing from Nikki, apparent confirmation that she's a no-show. Hopefully, this doesn't become a habit and I have to reprimand her for it. That's a challenge for another day.

Scrolling through my messages, I find my text thread with J, smiling to myself at our naughty back and forth. We usually save the deeper conversation for when we see each other in person, and that's okay with me.

My perspective on his interaction with Bianca began to shift as I got ready for work this morning. If I'm having a hard time accepting something uncomplicated and good in my life, that might be a *me* problem. And I know I deserve good things in my life, so why would I look a cosmic gift horse in the mouth and be ungrateful for it? If my boyfriend gets along with my little sister and my sister can tolerate him, I'm allowed to accept that. I *should*. I can even let myself enjoy that with unbridled happiness if I so choose.

And I *do* choose.

Thinking about you…you wore me out last night.

I send the text to J without allowing myself to do my usual overthinking. One minute goes by, then two. Then five.

A sigh erupts from my chest again. J's a busy man. I can't get annoyed if J doesn't immediately respond to my every text. He's shown time and again since we've been together that he cares.

So…not gonna worry about it. Nope.

As a matter of fact, since I ended up working up a real sweat during my pretend workout session, I'm just going to put my phone away to go freshen up a bit before I get my day started. Generally, I prefer going into meetings without looking damp and unkempt.

I swing by the front desk before I head to the restroom. By now, the hallways are buzzing with people and the usual office noise – printers printing, the camera crew in the filming room barking orders, the random snippets of different phone conversations I catch as I pass by open office doors.

"Morning, Gail." I walk up to the side of the large from desk area and grin at the receptionist. She's blonde and perky and always has a smile on her face that looks genuine – a rare thing in New York.

"Oh – hi, Brooklyn! You look so nice this morning."

I look down at my basic skirt and heels, shrugging a little. "Thanks. Listen, did Nikki leave any messages for me? I don't think she's made it in yet."

My wayward assistant is nowhere in the building and I know it, but I'd still like to protect her reputation. If I talk trash about Nikki to Gail, it'll be all over the office before lunch. Gail looks nice but she can't hold water.

She rifles through her stack of messages for a few seconds with pursed lips, then shakes her head. "Sorry, Brooklyn. I don't have any messages from her here for today. Maybe she called your direct phone?"

"Maybe," I say, nodding in agreement for her benefit. "Thanks."

Pushing off the counter, I head toward the restroom. I could always call her up and demand to know where Nikki is, but that would only increase the likelihood of a confrontation. That's the last thing I want.

She could actually be sick today. And even if she isn't, she deserves privacy as much as I do. I can give Nikki the benefit of the doubt. For now.

I'm not sure how far my grace will extend if the disappearing act goes on for too much longer.

I let my mind race while I do my business in the ladies' room, trying to get as many random anxieties and worries out of my system as possible before I need to be *on*. I can worry about all the other things later, when I don't have so much on my plate.

The universe decides I need to worry right now when I open the door and find Nikki standing at the sink directly across from my stall, her arms crossed like she's been waiting for me much longer than she would have liked.

My body freezes for an instant, the wind knocked out of me. I've spent so long imagining this moment ever since I received that little cardboard box, now that it's suddenly here, I…I'm finding it difficult to adjust.

Especially when I notice a strange gleam in Nikki's eyes I've never seen before. Almost predatory. As I watch her studying me in charged silence, I don't think she's blinked once. It's more than a little unsettling.

"Hey," I say, trying to keep my cool as I move to the sink to wash my hands, "where have you been all morning?" I keep watching her out of the corner of my eye. She still hasn't stopped smiling. Something about Nikki is super off today.

"Sorry I'm late," she says, her voice bright and bubbly – totally at odds with her outfit, which is jet black lace from head to toe. The only spot of color is the crimson red of her lips. She looks like a textbook femme fatale with her hair up in a bun and light eyes shrouded with dark eye shadow. Her eyes brighten when she meets mine in the mirror. "Did you get my gift?"

My throat goes dry and I have to swallow hard before I can speak again. I hadn't realized how much I've been dreading her asking me that question until it was hanging in the air.

"Um…" Lord, I need a minute. I take my time rinsing the vestiges of soap off my hands, shaking them out, patting them dry with a brown paper towel from the receptacle on the wall. "I…did receive it. But I'm not gonna lie; I'm not sure how I feel about it." That's as honest as I can be with her right now. This weird energy Nikki is putting off has me on my guard, though I can't put my finger on why.

Her hand lands gently on my shoulder and it takes everything in me not to recoil a bit. Not because I'm not attracted to her – looking at Nikki in this outfit in particular is making me feel some things – but because I don't know where she and I are or what we're doing, and I don't want our physicality to muddy the waters any more than they already have. But I don't pull away because I frankly don't know how she'll react.

"Brooklyn, look at me."

The soft, seductive quality of her voice compels me to obey, even though I'd rather look anywhere else. I have to take a deep breath first, but I do meet her eyes, and the new intensity I find there makes it hard to breathe altogether.

"Listen, I'm an adult. You and J are adults. We make adult decisions and we all decided to play together. There's nothing wrong with that, so don't feel bad or guilty about it, okay?"

My shoulders begin to relax. This has been a common refrain between us since our first sexual interaction at the BDSM club. Damn, it's something else hearing the same words I've been trying to make myself believe for the longest time coming from her lips. I hate that I needed the validation, but here we are. I already feel better.

Until Nikki's hand finds my hip and gives it a delicate squeeze. Desire rises up in me, so ferocious I feel a sudden pounding throb between my thighs that's just shy of painful.

Nikki leans in and I have no choice but to close my eyes and take in her nearness and delectable scent – peaches and brown sugar and hints of vanilla. Delicious and edible.

It makes my mouth water, muddling all my senses to the point I can barely think straight. All I want to do in this moment is pick her up, plop her down on the sink and dive face-first between her legs. Which is beyond the most insane thought I've ever had. What the fuck is wrong with me? Did she show up to the office dipped in pheromones or something?

When she speaks again, it's right in my ear. Slowly, so my delicate skin can absorb every word. Exactly the way J would do it, and it shakes me to the core. "Hey, you're my boss. I will always respect you, no matter what. But if you're attracted to me, Brooklyn, I think you should follow your instincts."

Oh, Nikki – that's so much easier said than done. I don't recognize myself in this moment. My assistant has apparently bottled the sexual energy that she brought to the club with J and I and has doused herself in it. I can't think straight. I can't see straight. All I know is this intense, pounding need to taste every part of her, and I don't know what the fuck to do with myself.

Best thing is not to touch her with my own hands, because I don't trust them. A take a step back and Nikki's hand slips off my shoulder. She lets it fall back to her side but I see her eyes wander my face.

I take another deep breath. Then another. Then that breath seizes in my chest when I realize someone could walk in here and catch us like this. We're not touching anymore, but any sane person would recognize the sexual energy crackling in the air like lightning about to strike. Not exactly suitable for work.

"Nikki," I say, clearing my throat when my voice cracks, "I don't think I need to remind you that we're at work right now. No matter what happens outside, we still have to be professional in here." The reminder is as much for myself as it is for her.

Nikki's eyes sparkle darkly, like she's hiding a dirty secret. She wets her matte red lips, leaving them glossy. "You don't have to worry about that."

"Good." I need to get back to my office, but I don't trust my wobbly legs to move until after Nikki leaves, so I have every intention of letting her go first. I don't know if she senses this or not, but she turns to leave right then.

I think I'm in the clear until she pauses halfway through the doorway. "I meant what I said in that note, Brooklyn – I want you to myself. And I'm not afraid to prove it."

And then she was gone, the door swinging shut in her wake. I have to brace myself on the sink for support. I'm not sure why that almost sounded like a threat, but God only knows how I'm going to make it through the rest of the day with Nikki working by my side.

Jesus Christ.

Four

I have never looked forward to a weekend more in my entire life.

Strangely, not for the reasons I thought I would. If anything, Nikki has never been more professional. I have coffee, meeting minutes, files – anything I need practically before I can ask for them. She's taken the standard for an assistant up a couple of notches and sustained it all week.

At the same time, however, Nikki has dialed the friendship side of our relationship all the way back. No chitchat. No inside jokes. She's in and out of my office with a bright smile when she needs to be there and not a minute longer. Nikki might be physically present, but I still find myself missing the warm sense of camaraderie between us. I could always rely on it, especially when either of us had had a particularly shitty day.

And then I'll catch that feline gleam in Nikki's eye time and again, reminding me of our interlude in the bathroom. Nothing else has gone down since that day, but a part of me that is increasingly difficult to suppress keeps screaming in frustration that it hasn't.

I want her. Badly. To the point that my usual text conversations with J have become a little awkward because I barely know what to say to him. I feel like I've been unfaithful even though I haven't done anything. He's been out of town for work and we haven't seen each other – and thank God for that, because I only have the emotional bandwidth to concentrate on one problem at a time this week.

Nikki is Perfect Patty until Friday comes, when she licks her lips and gives me a pointedly suggestive look as she leaves the office for the day.

I don't know what this girl has done to me, but I may or may not have rubbed one out every night to fantasies of she and I – and sometimes, the two of us along with J – and every single orgasm leaves me trembling and breathless and sick to my stomach with guilt.

I'm not proud of it.

At least I don't have to think about Nikki or our relationship for a couple of days with the arrival of the weekend. I fully intend to do everything I can to keep my hands and mind too busy to linger on the things they shouldn't, starting with tending to my family.

I made a promise to myself after my sister's incident that I would do a better job at being more present for the people I love, so I try to make good on that.

While I'm throwing breakfast together and still in my pajamas, I text Derrick because I know very well there's no way my twenty-five-year-old little brother is going to put up with an actual phone call from his sister.

Are you staying out of trouble, Big Head?

I finally hear back from him when I'm seated cross-legged in a chair at the kitchen table and almost done eating my eggs and toast.

I AM trouble, Dummy. Luv u

I already know that's about all I'm going to get out of him for today. I'm lucky to get that much. But it just makes me smile and finish off the last few sips of my coffee. At least I know he's okay.

Since I called my mom last night before I went to bed and she said she'd be running errands most of the day today, I know I'll see her tomorrow for our standing family dinner.

It's my sister I really want to spend some time with. With things going so well when Bianca hung out with J and I the other week, I want to be more deliberate about being around her. There's so much I feel like I don't know about her life. I'd like to get to know her as a whole person, not just my little sister.

I start to text her like I did our brother at first, but something compels me to reach out in such a way that I can hear her voice, get a real read on what she's feeling in the moment.

I dial her number and wait as the line rings. I'd let one of my legs swing freely; when I catch my foot tapping under the table, I force myself to stop. Am I actually nervous?

"Hello?"

I blink, surprised I didn't get her voicemail the way I had expected. "Oh! Uh, hey, B. It's your sister."

"God, I know who this is, Brooklyn." I can practically hear her eyeroll through the phone. "What's up?"

"Uh…" I bite my lip, catch myself, stop. "Do you have plans today?"

"Uh, *why?*" The way Bianca draws out the last word reeks of suspicion.

"Can't I want to spend time with my sister today? You make it seem like I'm trying to have you kidnapped or something." My cheeks warm as I scowl down at my phone. I don't know if I'm annoyed by her reaction or straight up offended.

"Well, you should have just said that, Brooklyn. It's not hard." I hear something like a car door slamming in the background. Sounds like she's already out.

"Why are you being so difficult, Bianca? All I wanted to do was ask if you want to go grab a coffee or something today."

She falls quiet for a moment, a little too long. The waiting makes me grit my teeth hard enough to pop my jaw. Is she punishing me for something?

Maybe this was a bad idea. Maybe it's just too soon to be trying to hang out as adult siblings outside of a crisis when it's been so long. There I go again, feeling like I'm adrift at sea without a paddle or a map, and I don't like it.

"Well, you didn't say coffee was involved at first – of course I can meet you." Bianca laughs. Like always, I want to strangle her and hug her in the same heartbeat. Still, I'm glad her sense of humor seems to have returned in full force since her ordeal.

We set a time and Bianca agrees to meet me at this cute little coffee spot that recently opened a few blocks from my apartment I've been wanting to try.

Before I clean up, I answer a check-in text from J – he's expecting to be back in town by mid-week. I wish him a safe trip and tell him to call me when he has some time to talk. I still don't know much about what J does for a living, but at this point in our relationship, I'm not going to push him to give me more than he's ready to. He's done the same for me.

I end up skipping back to my bedroom to get ready for the day and roll my eyes at myself. Maybe it's lame to be this excited about spending time with a younger sibling; maybe it isn't. I just plan on enjoying as much of this time as I can and letting my mind dwell on something that isn't going to drive me insane for once.

The coffee shop is all pastel candy colors and bubble-shaped fonts – adorable. I don't have to wait long once I get there; Bianca breezes in a few minutes after I find us a comfy booth near a window that's bathed in sunshine.

I call her name when I spot her come in and wave her over.

"Hey," Bianca says, and throws her arms around me in the biggest hug I can ever remember receiving from my normally reserved sister. My eyes widen in surprise but I quickly recover and hug her back just as hard. Maybe Bianca wants this just as much as I do?

"'Hey' yourself," I say into her hair, and there is an abundance of it on display today. She's taken her braids down to let her thick coils spring free. When she pulls away and smiles at me, I see they frame her face, making her look like a little cinnamon-skinned doll. I just want to pinch her cheeks. I don't, of course; I wouldn't put it past Bianca to deck me in full view of everyone in the building for making her feel like a little kid.

She looks good. Healthy. I've been watching her like a possessed hawk since I had to rescue her from the bus stop that night. The purplish shadows beneath her eyes have almost disappeared and it looks like she's put on a pound or two as well. With the hoodie and jeans she always wears, she looks like a standard New York college student pursuing the American dream.

Truthfully, I've been a bit nervous to bring it up again since I don't want to trigger her, but I still have questions about the night she spent at my apartment. I'm hoping this cozy environment will loosen her tight lips enough to give me some additional answers.

"Well, go ahead and sit down," I tell her, gesturing at the booth opposite mine.

"Don't mind if I do." Bianca slides into the seat, then looks around at the table empty of everything except a container of paper napkins. "Where's my drink?"

"They have a bunch of fancy lattes that taste like flowers here. I wanted to wait to see what you wanted if you felt like experimenting." I pull a paper menu out of my purse at my side and push it toward her on the table.

Bianca raises an eyebrow but opens it up, her dark eyes moving over the page. "That chocolate tea looks promising, whatever that is." She puts the menu down and blinks at me. "What're you getting?"

I don't take the menu since I made up my mind before I got here. "I'm gonna do the rose latte. In a fancy mood today."

Bianca chuckles. "Ooh la la."

I smirk at her and raise the little flag next to our booth. A few minutes later, a lanky young man in jeans and a t-shirt sidles up to our table. "Hi, what can I get you guys?"

After I put in our order, the kid smiles and puts our flag down again before shuffling back to the front counter.

"So?" Bianca folds her hands on the table and stares at me, cocking her head. "I'm here. What's up?"

Now's the time. "I just wanna talk."

Her eyes narrow. "About…anything in particular?"

I swallow hard. "You never really talked about the guy you told me you followed to that party…" I trail off when I watch her entire body bristle. I almost don't have the heart to finish my sentence, but I know I have to stay the course if I want this conversation to have any chance at being productive. "Well, we were talking a little bit about relationships when you were at my house, and I was just wondering what yours had been like before…before the party."

I lick my lips and hold my breath as I wait for her answer.

Bianca doesn't speak for a long time and her gaze drifts off as I continue to watch her. I hope I haven't said the one thing that will make her shut down. Speaking to her sometimes feels like tiptoeing through a mine field.

And just my luck – our drinks show up right at that moment. The same host places our respective orders in front of us on the table and disappears again.

Ripping the paper wrapper off the straw, I take a sip of mine while I wait for Bianca to get her thoughts together. The first hit on my tongue makes me close my eyes – it's wonderful. Exotic, sweet and floral. I'm in love already. I'll have to bring J here once he gets back.

But now is not the time to think on my own love life. I continue to wait while Bianca tastes her drink. "How is it?"

"It's *really* good."

"Right? I had a feeling about this place." It's small talk in this context and honestly, I'm not loving it.

"His name was Xavier," Bianca finally says, her voice powder-soft as she studies her cup instead of looking at me. She can look wherever she wants. I'm just glad she's talking to me about this.

She pauses for so long I hurry to jump in and encourage her to keep talking. "Where did you meet him?" I take a sip of my drink and glance around the shop, trying to keep the pressure off my sister.

"American Lit. He missed a couple of classes early on in the semester and I let him borrow my notes." A wistful smile touches her lips but I don't think she realizes it.

"Okay. What did you like about him?"

"He was smart. Like, sharp with it, you know?" She finally makes eye contact and I nod like a horse in agreement. "And he wasn't a snob like a lot of the other students that go there, even though he comes from money." That small smile disappears.

"Did he treat you well?"

"He did, at first. But it got weird after a while." Bianca sits up straighter, rolling her shoulders.

My heart stops. "Weird how?"

Anger flashes across Bianca's face. "Why? Why are we even talking about this? I just wanted to drink my coffee and talk about…celebrity gossip, or something."

"We can do that," I say, my words rushing together in my hurry to get them out and reassure her. "I just wanted a better understanding on what you went through."

After a moment, Bianca sighs hard. "He got controlling, I guess. Told me who to hang out with, what and when I could eat, that kind of stuff. The more I liked him, he could tell. I'd do almost anything just to keep him talking to me. If I didn't do what he wanted, he'd ghost me and I'd feel like I was losing my mind every time. I hated it."

This boy was emotionally abusing her. I'm — I want to kill him with my bare hands. But Bianca dispatched this idiot on her own, strong young woman that she is. She doesn't need me getting all in my feelings and making her relive the emotional nightmare if she doesn't have to.

My hands are shaking under the table so hard I have to clench them together. "So, you walked away from him." I don't phrase it like a question because that's what she told me that night, when she was still partially drunk. I only hope it was the truth.

Bianca's gaze is clear and steady now. "I did. Left him at that party, blocked him, and cut him out of my life."

My grin stretches from ear to ear. "I'm proud of you. There's lots of women twice your age who wouldn't have had the strength to do what you did. I didn't when I was your age." I raise my plastic cup in a toast.

Bianca's brows shoot up just before she offers me the sweetest lopsided smile. She picks up her cup and taps it against mine. "Thanks."

We each take sips of our drinks and I let the warmth of this moment of real connection wash over me. It's stupid I waited this long to prioritize this. I suppose I didn't expect hanging out with Bianca to feel this nourishing.

"So…I didn't know you had a Jamaican boyfriend."

I feel like I've been hit with a blast of icy air – reality. "Neither did I." I take another sip of my drink and check out the balloon décor hanging from the ceiling. I'm still a little salty about J's little revelation. We still haven't talked about it.

Bianca's face screws up. "He never told you where his family is from?"

I shake my head. "Not that in particular."

"Interesting." She sips again, longer this time. Bianca was serious about finding her drink tasty. "So, how much do you actually know about him? Besides the obvious, like he's fine enough to have his own swimsuit calendar."

A laugh hits me so suddenly, I almost shoot liquid out of my nose and cough violently instead. My sister's laughter is clear and free, though it's more like a witch's cackle than anything else. "We're still getting to know each other," I say when I can talk again.

"I bet you're having fun with that process."

I start to protest but Bianca can hardly hear me, she's laughing so hard at her own lewd commentary. I had no idea she had such a dirty sense of humor, but I think I'm enjoying it more than I could have expected. The sparkle that has returned to her eyes makes me happiest of all.

"Yeah, okay – can you go get us one of those desserts in the case? I think there was a green tea bun or something shaped like a pig."

"Ooh, really?" Bianca's face lights up like she's five years old again and I have to bite back a smile. She still loves sweets. "Be right back."

I'm about to grab my phone to check my messages when Bianca stops in her tracks a few steps from the table. She looks at me over her shoulder and grins. "I'm glad we did this."

My smile is a reflection of hers. "Me, too."

She bounces off to get our treats and I try to make quick work thumbing through my texts. I had my phone on silent so I didn't get distracted. It worked, because I see I missed, what, eight messages?

J must really miss me. Biting my lip in anticipation, I tap with my thumb to expand the messages so I can see the sender.

My face falls when I see photo after nude photo of Nikki, followed by a row of "shush" emojis. If J were to see these...

Shit.

Five

"**D**errick, if you drop those tomatoes after I just washed them, I'm gonna drop kick *you* out the front door."

As usual, my little brother just grins and ignores my empty threats, eyes on the round red fruits he's juggling in the kitchen – the same ones I've been trying for the last few minutes to chop for our side salad. Mom put my siblings and I to work doing all the prep for our family dinner this week since she had some stuff to finish in her office upstairs. Pretty difficult to accomplish when all Derrick wants to do today is clown around.

My arms may be crossed but I can never manage to stay mad at my little brother for long, even when he's being annoying. I hold out my hand with a roll of my eyes instead. "Come on, D – do you see a circus around here? You're not being paid."

Derrick keeps smiling up at the ceiling, eyes glued to the tomatoes miraculously staying aloft with each quick move of his hands. Where'd he even learn to do that? His bare feet are silent on the kitchen tile as he moves around, trying to dodge me each time I swipe an arm at him to throw off his balance.

"Who says I'm not? Your irritation is pretty entertaining. That's payment enough in my book."

The bark of laughter behind me makes me turn my glare on Bianca, who shakes her head as she pulls a pan of rolls from the oven to cool on the stovetop. My sister tries to angle the pan away from me to hide the too-brown edges, but I give her a dirty look so she knows I saw them. I told her she had the oven temperature too high in her efforts to "make the baking go quicker", but she didn't want to listen to me.

I could make a big deal out of our half-burnt side dish, but I won't. Bianca and I have been in such a good place since our little coffee outing a couple weeks back, I don't want to rock the boat over something petty and unimportant.

We've talked either via text or phone every day since then. Honestly, I still can't believe it's working, because part of me expected her to want to disengage at any moment, for us to go back to the way we were. Like distant relatives with no real substance to the relationship.

Once I realized that's not what I wanted, I was all-in. I didn't wait for Bianca to reach out to me after we parted ways at the coffee shop. I hit her up the very next day, kept it light, sent her some funny meme or something just to keep the conversation going. I was worried she'd see my efforts as some kind of ploy and not see my heart, how much I wanted to have a better relationship with her. The first few times I sent her a text or called I felt like I was going to shit myself. But it worked, and the next thing I knew we were chatting all the time about her dating life throughout high school and how things had changed for her once she got to college, even about the kind of life she wanted for herself once she graduated.

And the adult version of my little sister is so *funny*. She's just as goofy as Derrick but her humor is, shall we say, a little more sophisticated. She's the queen of the double-entendre and has left me cackling until my throat was sore more than once.

I adore her. She's deep and conscientious and so smart. Now that she's even started to ask for advice here and there, I don't ever want to give up having that position in her life now that I've earned it.

Being the big sister in Derrick's life is still a work in progress. He taps me on the back, finally placing the tomatoes into my hands with an innocent smile. I love my brother to death, but it's gonna take a lot more time and patience for me to get there with him. And that's okay. Right now, however, all we have to do is sit down to a meal together and have a good time.

They both help me set the table while we wait for Mom to come back downstairs and join us. Derrick and I have each tripped Bianca once and are still laughing at her little indignant stumbles by the time our mother arrives. I guess juvenile behavior is contagious tonight.

We're still giggling when Mom gives Derrick and I an appraising look after we all sit down and start filling our plates from the various ceramic bowls of food on the table. "Did you slip some bourbon in this iced tea, Brooklyn?"

My head tips back when I laugh. "I could use a drink, but no." I wink at Bianca, who is still faking a scowl, and Derrick seated next to me gives me a fist pound under the table. "I guess I'm just really happy to be with my family tonight."

Mom grins wider than I've seen in a long time. "I can drink to that!" You would have thought there *was* liquor in her tea by the way she clinked all our raised glasses in turn with such gusto.

Seated next to me, Derrick shoots me a questioning glance that reflects my own thoughts. What's up with her tonight?

I have no idea, but I'm gonna find out. She's been unusually chipper the last few weeks, but Mom has been mum whenever any of us would ask what she had going on. I'm feeling emboldened by the repair of the family fabric, so I look my mother in the eye. "Mommy, what's going on with you lately?" I waggle my fingers at her and she raises her eyebrows. "This glow you have these days doesn't have anything to do with your job…does it?"

"Young lady, I'll have you know my career is very fulfilling and you should mind your business," she says, but the way her mouth quirks I can tell she's trying hard not to laugh.

"Come on, Mom," Bianca says to her with a nod of agreement at me, "I've noticed it, too. Like it or not, you've been acting weird."

Having turned toward Bianca, Mom's eyes go wide. "Weird? Whatever do you mean?" Her gaze moves to Derrick. "Do you know what they're talking about, son?"

Derrick immediately puts up both hands in surrender and looks away from all of us. "Nope – I ain't in it." He rips a chunk off one of Bianca's hard rolls with his teeth and makes himself busy chewing.

Mom laughs again then folds her arms in her lap once she settles down, eyes sparkling like topaz, full of warmth and secrets. Good secrets, I hope.

I stop breathing when she speaks again. "Well…I did kind of…meet someone."

"I knew it!" Bianca smacks her hand down on the wood tabletop so hard I worry for second she's hurt herself for real before relieved laughter bubbles up in my chest and spills out of me. So, my sophisticated mother has been waltzing around here like a teenager with a crush because she's in love?

I might be smiling but Bianca looks terrified, and my glance at Derrick reveals he might be considering homicide, which is worrisome. We need to get details before either of my siblings do something stupid.

"So…" With my hand out, I roll my wrist to encourage the flow of information, but my mother doesn't bite.

"'So' what?" She bats her long lashes at me and I want to growl in frustration.

"Do we get to know his name or what? What does he do for a living? Where'd you meet him? How old is he? *Who* is he?"

"Whoa, whoa – slow down!" With her eyes closed and her hands up, Mom looks like she wants to back away from the table altogether, but she eventually relaxes once she sees how serious we all suddenly are. "Fine, since y'all are so *concerned*…his name is Tony – Anthony – and he's one of the psychology professors at my school."

"And how long have you known this man?" Bianca leans in toward Mom, not even blinking.

Mom leans back slightly. "We've known each other in a professional capacity for about three years, but we've been seeing each other socially for about a year."

"Mom! You've been dating this guy for a whole year and you haven't said anything to any of us?" A vein has popped out in Derrick's forehead; the kid is going to blow a gasket if he doesn't calm down.

"D, relax…it's not the end of the world." With a hearty squeeze to Derrick's shoulder, I say those words as much for myself as for Derrick and Bianca. There hasn't been a significant male presence in this house since our parents split when we were all still young and our father moved on without us. For most of our lives, it's only been us and Mom. This marks a huge shift in our family dynamic and I can't pretend nothing will change if our mother intends on incorporating this guy into our life.

That said, I need to set the example here. Our mother is a human being who deserves to be happy, not just the woman who's birthed and cared for us all. She deserves her moment without us making her feel bad about it.

I turn back to Mom and her creased brow, trying my best to keep the train of this evening's festivities from derailing. "I think Derrick just wants to know if he's nice and treats you well, Mom."

The tension eases from her tight features. "He does, baby. Opens my door, brings me lunches he cooked himself so we can eat together, buys me flowers almost every day. He's a perfect gentleman. I just…" Her gaze drops to her lap and she trails off, fiddling with her fingers in a nervous gesture I've never seen from her before. "I just wanted to be sure how I felt about him before I introduced him to you all. I know it's a big change and I didn't want anyone coming in and out of your life, even though you're all adults now. Do you understand?"

She's talking to all of us but she's looking at Derrick, whose downcast eyes and frown make him appear as if he's just lost his best friend. He and our mother have always been so close, I know my brother probably feels like his special position is in danger of being taken.

With our collective reaction to the news, I can't blame our mother for being secretive about her relationship up until now. It stings she didn't tell us after so long, but Lord knows she still hasn't met J yet, and I don't think any of us knew anything about Bianca's relationship before that fiasco at the bus stop. With the casual way Derrick is with his women, I doubt he's been into anyone seriously, but what do I know? This revelation from our own parent is proof positive I don't know shit about anyone.

Mom must feel the same way, because she asks Derrick, "And what's going on with *you*? You haven't really talked to us about school in a while."

Just like that, Bianca and I are looking at our brother instead of our mother and the subject is changed. Very smooth.

Now that the attention is on him, I fully expect Derrick to give some flippant response and change the subject yet again. I can tell he wants to get more info on this new boyfriend from Mom, but he doesn't push it.

Instead, he seems to transform into a young man I've never met right before my eyes.

His gaze seems to turn inward and pensive. "Actually, it's funny you should ask that. I, uh, took this random photography class when I needed an extra elective for my degree this semester and…it's been kind of lifechanging."

I feel my mouth drop open in shock and have to snap it closed. He's *never* said stuff like that. Derrick is the type of guy to bullshit his way through college just to have something to do since he bores so easily, but this evident self-introspection is a whole new quality. Bianca and I stare at him like he's grown a second head, but Mom just smiles and encourages him to tell us more.

He goes on, his raspy voice soft, like he's embarrassed to be talking about it at all. "It's a photography history class based on studying the impact photography has made on human culture. I thought it was going to be really dumb, but…I've learned so much it's made get my own camera."

Bianca actually gasps. "You bought a camera? To take *pictures?*"

Derrick narrows his eyes at her. "Obviously."

I can sense the tension in his body ramping up, so I hurry and ask more questions before an argument can break out. "That's amazing, D. What kind of things are you focusing on for your photography?" And I honestly want to know; I've never seen Derrick with any sense of real direction. Witnessing this kind of passion in him come out of nowhere is beyond fascinating.

His face brightens at my question. "I want to shine light on serious issues, you know? The plight of the homeless, addiction, stuff like that. I went with a friend of mine to a shelter a few months ago and you wouldn't believe some of the stories I heard from the people down there." He swallows so hard I can see his Adam's apple bob in his throat. "*Hearing* about it is one thing; *seeing* it is something else. You can't ignore something in your face. I feel like…if people could see the horrors that are right in their backyard, they might actually do something to help."

The rest of us at the table fall into stunned silence. I have no idea who this new version of Derrick is that has suddenly revealed himself, but…I definitely want to get to know him so much better than I do right now.

Mom is so beside herself with happiness to hear the direction her only son's life has taken, she's about to wriggle right out of her highbacked chair. "That is *so wonderful,* baby! I'm so proud of you. I've always known you were talented in your own way."

I giggle when I notice the proud male in our family actually *blushing.* Hilarious.

"Well," Bianca says, "you do realize that you have officially made yourself the family photographer for the rest of our lives, right? Vacations, passport photos, fake ID's – that's all on you. And I will *not* be paying a dime, got it?"

Derrick snorts in disbelief, but his smile looks borne of relief to me. "We'll talk when the time comes. I believe more in the barter system."

That just makes us all laugh, the tension easing around the table all at once. I could really go for that drink now.

Mom must be on a similar wavelength, because she stands up with a definitive clap of her hands. "On that note, I think I'll cut the cake."

Bianca's ears perk up. "You made a cake? What kind? Where is it?" Her head swivels on her neck as she searches the kitchen around her and comes up empty.

"It's a lemon pound cake and I hid it so you wouldn't go taking nibbles before dinner," Mom says as she heads to the breadbox tucked into a corner on the counter that none of us ever bother to look inside since it's usually empty.

"Oh, well played," Derrick says with a chuckle at Bianca's pout. A wise decision on Mom's part, but I don't get a chance to tell her before the doorbell rings and throws me off completely. It's too late for a delivery, so it has to be the boyfriend. I played it cool when she told us about him, but that definitely doesn't mean I'm ready to meet the guy *tonight*.

I share my worried look with Bianca. I'm doubly concerned when I find Bianca's smirk just before she jumps up to get the door.

What the hell is that about?

Derrick is preoccupied with being first in line for the pound cake, so he's absent from his chair when I turn to him for emotional support. Alone at the table, I grab my glass and take a sip of iced tea. I hope to everything and everyone holy I am not about to meet my potential future stepfather.

That sip of tea rushes right into my lungs when I gasp at the sight of J walking into my mother's kitchen with three rose bouquets wrapped in tissue paper nestled in the crooks of his arms.

"Oh, Brooklyn – take it easy, there!" Treacherous-ass Bianca pats my back way too hard as I work my way through my coughing fit, bent over double in my chair and gulping down breaths like I'm dying.

What the fuck is happening? Did she plan this? Did they plan it together?

My hacking springs tears to my eyes and through my suddenly bleary vision I see J standing at the opposite end of the table, grinning at me like the cat who ate the canary.

I see him, I heard him speak to me, but I still don't believe it.

I can't even acknowledge him in my shock, which is just as well — my mom has just turned from the kitchen counter at the commotion with a squeak of surprise at our very unexpected guest. Who knows what Derrick's reaction is to all this considering how he felt about a new man in our mother's life, but I don't have time to worry about him. Instead, I turn in my seat to speak to my sister under my breath. "Bianca…" I sound hoarse to my own ears when I'm finally able to talk again. "What the hell is J doing here? He never said anything to me about showing up tonight." I absolutely know she has something to do with it, but I'm not sure how and I need her to say it out loud. Maybe then I could make sense of it, but it's not going to stop me from wanting to strangle her like I do right now.

Bianca rolls her eyes like she's annoyed I asked the question. "Why are you so freaked out? We exchanged numbers when we were at your apartment. I figured he might as well meet everybody at once."

She shrugs and heat blooms in my body as I grit my teeth. I love Bianca more than anything, but…this is too much. She has completely overstepped. Where does she get off making a decision like this *for me*?

I purse my lips and let out a slow breath. I owe baby sis a conversation in short order about boundaries, but now isn't the time. The adult version of our sisterhood and friendship is so new that that particular convo requires some delicacy – and privacy. Neither of which I have at the moment.

No, right now I need to deal with my boyfriend, who is handing over one of his bouquets to my mom and laughing when she squeals in delight and throws an arm around his shoulder in a half-hug.

It's one thing for J to show up at my house out of concern for myself and my sister. It's another for him to show up at my *mother's* house without a word to me on the subject. Of course, it's something I wanted to have happen in the near future, but we never had a discussion about it happening in real time. He didn't ask how I felt about it, he just…arrived with a smile like it was no big deal.

I didn't give the okay for this! How dare he take away the choice and the opportunity to invite him here to my family's private domain?

I'm so hot I find myself dabbing away sweat from my upper lip with a trembling hand. The family's collective gaze finally registers, however, and feels like ice water down my back.

"Well, I certainly wasn't expecting a guest tonight, but this is definitely a pleasant surprise!" My mother looks as excited as she does confused, her eyes wide and expectant as she looks from J to Bianca to myself. Bianca has apparently found the fridge extremely interesting and doesn't look my way. How convenient.

Well, shit — not like a have any choices if I don't want to look any more ridiculous in front of my family than I'm sure I already do.

Bracing my hands on my somewhat wobbly knees, I push myself to a stand and gesture at J.

"J, this is my family. Family, this is J…my boyfriend."

$\mathcal{Six}$

I feel like a guest at my own mother's kitchen table.

The minute I officially introduce J as my boyfriend, Mom is beside herself – hugging him, fussing over him, asking if he's eaten then dismissing his answer and insisting he sit down so she can make him a plate of our dinner.

I've barely looked at J. Anyone with good vision can probably make out the steam pouring out of my ears. The time or two I've hazarded a glance at him since he showed up unannounced and uninvited, J didn't even have the grace to look the least bit contrite. Just smiled at me like this was totally normal. Like our relationship wasn't rooted in some strangeness I'm still trying to reconcile.

This brownstone and the people in it are *mine,* goddammit. Mine. Always have and always will be. He does not have the right to show up at family events without discussing it with me, no matter what my little sister told him. He should know better than that.

I may have introduced him as my boyfriend, but we'll see how long that lasts.

He eats and I try not to strangle him with my eyes. I feel Bianca's heavy gaze but I don't look her way, either. I don't want her to think all this animus is for her when she's only earned a little of it.

How dare you – where do you get off – you never said anything to me – do I show up at your *parents' house unannounced?* The words I want to say but can't crowd my mouth to the point I have to press my lips together to keep them in. I don't want to cause a scene and draw into question my dating choices, especially with my mom.

She keeps needling for more info, though. Mom tag-teams with my siblings – even Derrick has reappeared at the table to get in on the action – and they give J the third degree. I've never seen such efficient teamwork between them, but they don't know they're dealing with a professional. J dodges and weaves and gives beautiful, noncommittal answers that leave them all vaguely unsatisfied. *I* know why – I've felt that way more times than I can count since J and I met. It makes no sense he's not a politician; he'd be great at it.

Doesn't seem to matter. I continue to sit in silence and observe, dodging the questioning glances I've started to receive from J. By the time J has cleaned his plate, my mother is giggling and leaning into his arm like he's her new son-in-law, Bianca sits across from me wearing that smug smirk, and I even catch a grunt that sounds like some kind of approval from Derrick.

I don't care about anyone's fucking approval tonight but mine, and J didn't get it before he barged into this part of my life without the one person's opinion that should have mattered to him the most.

I've never been more relieved for one of our family dinners to end. Everyone says their goodbyes and begins to make their way to the door, with my mom telling J to make sure he doesn't stay a stranger.

Bianca takes her flowers with her, but I leave mine on the kitchen table, untouched.

J stands beside me in the hallway. "Hey, is everything okay?"

It most certainly is *not.* "We can talk outside." My words sound clipped to my own ears as we follow Derrick and Bianca outside and down the front steps.

"Bye!" I call out to them both after our parting embraces and wave high over my head. "Text me when you get home!"

My smile vanishes and my entire body recoils and jerks away the moment J's hand touches my elbow. Can't say I'm entirely prepared for the stricken look that crosses his face when he turns toward me on the sidewalk.

"What is your problem? You haven't said a word to me since I got here."

He offers a half smile but the tightness around his eyes suggests genuine hurt. I can't lie; it makes my stomach twist with anxiety just a little. But so what? I'm hurt, too. I thought we were further along in our relationship than this. This dinner set us back so far I don't care how he feels right now. He's the one who violated tonight.

"You…didn't tell me you were coming beforehand. You never said anything about it." My retort sounded way spicier in my head. Out loud it sounds lame, but I've already committed to being pissed off and I plan to see this through. I cross my arms and try my best to look dangerous.

J bristles, the muscles in his arms flexing beneath his polo shirt. That little smile disappears completely with the arrival of a full-on frown. "I guess you're not familiar with the concept of a surprise." When I bite my lip and keep glaring up at him, he shakes his head. "I don't understand – it was *your* sister who reached out to me. I honestly thought you had something to do with the invitation. Excuse me for thinking you *wanted* me here to meet the rest of your family."

Ugh. That's…not an unreasonable assumption, but that's the point – it was an *assumption*. J didn't ask me. He took liberties he hasn't earned yet.

The glare J levels at me makes my resolve falter. "Huh."

That's all he says, and the brevity without any elaboration sends my anger surging back in a hot, heavy wave. "What?"

"This is starting to feel like you didn't believe me when I said I wanted to try to have a real relationship with you."

That's not what I expected him to say, and I find myself having to blink at him until my brain can catch up enough to spout a rebuttal.

Clearing my throat, I cross my arms more tightly across my chest. "What are you talking about?" It's not much, but it's all I got.

J mirrors my stance and a sudden lump in my throat makes it hard to swallow. "As I recall, you were the one who said that's what you wanted. Something real. Something more traditional." His mouth curls in the corner, turning his expression into something bitter and painful to witness. "Isn't meeting your family part of that?"

It is. It should be…the truth gnaws at me in the form of an uncomfortable tug low in my belly. Now I can't keep still and shift from foot to foot. "Look, the bottom line is that you keep trying to control the situation, and I don't like that shit."

His brows shoot up. "What are you talking about? Because I showed up at your apartment to make sure you and your sister were okay? You wanted me to call first?" J grunts and shakes his head. "Brooklyn, that's fucking stupid."

"*You're* fucking stupid!" The words are out of my mouth before I can snatch them back, juvenile and ugly and pointless. But now that I've said it, I can't back down lest both of us start believing I have no spine. "You have no right to decide if and when you can show up in *my* personal spaces to meet *my* family." I'm shaking so hard now I have to clench my teeth to keep speaking normally. "Checking on me at my place is one thing. Showing up at my *mother's* house unannounced? That's crossing the line. I wouldn't have done that to you." I'm tired of that runaway train feeling in my own life. I'm tired of people I care about, however well they might mean, making decisions for me.

J looks away toward the street, staring at nothing. People and cars move past us in both directions in the ceaseless dance of the inner city. I stand there in silence and let the amber streetlights wash over me, hoping the pause will shed some light on what else I can say to make him understand the frustration I've been feeling.

"So," J begins again, his voice hoarser than the last time he spoke, "all that stuff you said was bullshit, then."

My eyes close when my body flinches at his cold tone and even colder words. "No, but I can tell you what you've been doing lately isn't what I want. You can't dictate the terms of our relationship, J."

"Well, somebody has to start moving in that direction since you don't seem to know what you want."

Excuse me?

When I open my mouth this time, my voice is loud enough to catch the curious eyes of passersby. "How the fuck would you know? You trying to control my feelings now, too?" A humorless laugh escapes my lips. "Maybe I should have listened to Nikki; she said your ass was controlling."

J's dark eyes flash and I immediately back up a step-in response. His full lips tighten into a thin line. His hands clench into tight fists at his sides but he comes no closer. What is he going to do? Put his hands around my throat? No, J would never hurt me. The basest parts of me still like that idea a lot, but my anxious thinking mind is worried this may be the argument that ends us for good. I don't think I've ever seen him this angry.

My chest heaves as I watch him and wait, hoping he doesn't drop a bomb on me.

He takes a deep breath then, closes his eyes, then gives me a look of warning that chills me to the bone marrow. "I'm only going to say this once: Nikki is dangerous. I've known her long enough to know she's poison. Keep fucking around with her and you'll find out soon enough." With a parting glare, J turns on his heel and stalks down the street away from me before I can make a retort.

Which is probably for the best, because in no way did I expect him to say that. I would have likely just stared like a deer in headlights if he had stuck around to finish the conversation. Because it *wasn't* finished.

What did his swift exit mean, anyway? Was that his way of breaking up? Were we just on a break?

As I stand there staring down the street where J has long since disappeared, my pulse continues to thrum through my veins. My heart is pounding so hard my head has started to hurt. The thought of J no longer being in my life is unthinkable, but the fear of losing my voice in my romantic relationship is something I can't bear. I've done it before, borne the consequences, and swore to myself I'd never do it again. I have every intention of keeping that promise to myself if nothing else, but…I don't know what I want now when it comes to J and I.

Perhaps he was right about that.

I'm too upset after my argument with J to stay the night with my mom for a little slumber party the way I'd intended, so I take my tired ass home to my lonely apartment instead. It's late by the time I get there and I'm still feeling too low to blast some music and turn on all the lights the way I usually do. Nothing cheers me up as I toss my keys into the bowl by the door – not the silhouettes of my new houseplants hanging out on the sill of my large picture window, nor the delicate scent of orange blossoms in the air from my diffuser on the kitchen table. I bypass the living room TV and couch and opt to drag myself down the hall to my bedroom in shadow, with nothing but the minimal illumination from the nightlights under my kitchen cabinetry to light my way.

I don't even try to resist pulling out my phone to see if J has reached out to apologize. I've already checked ten times between here and my mom's house and have been met with a gut punch of disappointment every time I didn't see a single text or missed call from him. He's never done this before. And we've argued plenty in the past.

Throwing myself across the bed after kicking my shoes off into a corner, I wake up my phone and blink at the bright screen. My anger has faded into a nebulous kind of discomfort, and honestly, I can barely remember why I was so mad at him in the first place. J didn't do anything *wrong*, per se, beyond allowing an egregious lack of communication. What man has never done that? I'd say I had a better one than most when it comes to that up until today.

Had.

Past tense.

My stomach trembles and I roll into a ball on my side after closing the screen on my phone again and staring blindly into the dark. God, I hope not.

But he's got another thing coming if he thinks I'm going to reach out to him first. Whether he'd had good intentions or not, J is the one who crossed the line and did wrong here, not me. He owes me an apology, and nothing about how we ended our conversation suggests he felt the least bit sorry for offending me the way he did. *That's* the shit that's not going to fly.

With a sigh, I grab my phone to check it again, knowing what I'll see – or rather, what I won't – and still not being able to keep myself from giving in to the compulsion. I bite my lip as the screen's brightness hits my pupils once again, making me squint.

Nothing. Of course.

Fucking bastard. How dare he act like I'm the one with the problem?

The next time I happen to check the time, I've been lying on my bed for an hour in the same position. I don't know why I thought I'd actually be able to sleep with all these abrasive thoughts coursing through my mind.

Had this been an issue with a friend or with someone at work, I would have called Bianca right now. Our sisterhood has matured to the point that I know her habits pretty well – she tends to stay up way later than I do and her phone is practically grafted to her hand at all times – and she would have happily given me a listening ear to vent.

I can't about this.

Despite J and I being currently on the outs, I don't want to dump this on her. I'd be lying to myself if I said there isn't a part of me that wants to be with J. Most of me, really. My body still cries out for him, even now, when I'm still pissed and the thought of seeing his face makes me want to throw something. Bianca seems to have developed a very positive impression of him, which is more than I could have ever asked for. I don't want to forever taint him in her eyes. If we reconcile – and I hope we do, one way or another – I know Bianca will never forgive him if she knows all the details about our disagreement. She'll side with me no matter what.

Calling Derrick is a moot point, so I sigh again and scroll through my contacts for the phone number of someone I know can offer some sound advice at such a late hour.

The line rings and I hold my breath.

"Hello?"

My friend's voice sounds groggy and slurred and my chest instantly tightens with guilt. "Hey, Sherry. Sorry I woke you up, girl."

I hear the muffled shuffle of what sounds like rustling bedsheets before she coughs to clear her throat. "Oh, hey Brooklyn…it's fine; I just fell asleep. What's going on? What's wrong?"

"Um…" I sigh. "I'm really sorry to bother you, but I wanted to get your advice about a…situation."

The sheets rustle loudly again, likely Sherry sitting up in bed to listen to my bullshit like the good friend she's always shown herself to be. "A man problem?"

My chuckle sounds strained and sad. "You know me very well."

Sherry's chuckle just sounds amused, so my bunched-up shoulder muscles start to relax. "Alright, then – lay it on me. What happened?"

I take a deep breath and do just that, talking and talking and talking, with more intensity than I thought I had the energy for. I lay it all out, hiding nothing. No matter how messy it might be, I'm hoping Sherry knows me well enough to pick through it all and let me know whether or not my sense of self-righteousness is out of place. The seed of doubt at J's reaction to my being so upset at the way he's been moving lately has sprouted like a weed during this call. More than anything, I want to know if I'm misinterpreting things because I can't get out of my feelings when it comes to J.

The second after I've purged to Sherry, the guilt rushes in again like a wave. "I'm sorry…I don't mean to dump all this on you randomly in the middle of the night."

"Listen," Sherry says, "don't even worry about it. You forgot how many times I called you just like this over my man problems back in the day?"

I laugh aloud at that. She's right – there were so many times over the years when she called me crying about some sorry ass dude doing her wrong. And I always told her that she was better than the bullshit she put up with and encouraged her to kick them to the curb, post haste.

"You were always a good friend to me, Brooklyn. Don't forget that."

"Thanks, Sherry." My chest warms with affection and appreciation instead of anger for the first time tonight. "I appreciate that."

"Anyway, I can understand where you've coming from when it comes to your man overstepping boundaries, but…I'm confused on exactly why you were so upset if you told him you wanted to be in a relationship. Isn't meeting your family a logical next step, even if he jumped the gun a little bit?"

"I was honest with him when I told him that. That's how I felt at the time." Even now, I don't know if something has changed since then to make me feel differently or if I was never clear with myself about what I wanted from the beginning – even before I met J.

A pang of clarity hits me like the peal of a gong. It's all this shit with Nikki complicating everything. Shit.

I don't dare tell Sherry that; it's too much for one night and I'm still working through that spider's web on my own.

"And how do you feel now?"

Things have never been murkier. "I don't know. I know he meant well, but there's a part of me that keeps resisting moving forward and I'm not sure why."

"If you could boil down how you felt after he showed up at your mom's house tonight, what would it be?"

I say it instantly. "Violated."

"Okay," Sherry says slowly, considering. "But why such a strong word if you're in a relationship with this person?"

"Because," I say, sitting up in bed as things start to become clearer and clearer, "he keeps pushing himself deeper and deeper into my life and sooner than I expected him to, Sherry. He's not asking me anything, planning anything *with* me ahead of time – he just *shows up.* Whether I'm ready for it or not." I pull my legs up against my chest and balance my phone on my knees so I can talk hands-free. "I want to be with him but I want to go at a pace I feel comfortable with. I'm not pushing *him.* I still know little to nothing about his people and his life when the two of us aren't together."

"And how long have y'all been official?"

"Less than a year." Not that long in the grand scheme of things.

"So…you're uncomfortable now because he's pushing to know more about you than you do about him?"

I let Sherry's question settle over me, and before I know it, the sentiment fits me like a tailored coat. "Yeah, that sounds about right."

"So why has he stopped answering your questions about his life?"

"I…" The answer dies in my throat when I realize what she's asked me. "I think I stopped asking the questions, now that I think about it."

"And why is that?"

"I'm usually on defense when it comes to my own life. I guess I want to reveal things on my own time, and every time I turn around, he's just…there, finding shit out on his own without my being able to tell him."

"Well," Sherry says, "when it comes to understanding how you feel, that right there is the thread you want to pull."

She's right, of course. But after tonight, I'm not sure I even want the answers to all those questions I had for him before.

Seven

One day slips into the other after family dinner. Eat, sleep, work, repeat. And I don't hear from J at all. No text, no call. Not even an email.

I can't decide if I'm pissed or worried to death. He's never gone this long without contact and something about his silence leaves me on edge. The first day or so after we had it out at my mother's house, it felt realer than ever and more than once I actually felt like we were broken up. I'm a woman who requires true closure for something like that, however. I need an official proclamation that we are done and over with before my heart and body can move on from a person.

Because of this realization about myself, by day two it felt more like a break than a breakup and I went right back to being pissed. Once again, J was trying to control the narrative and I'm just not going to allow that anymore.

It's been nearly a week since we've talked, and every part of my being is crying out from missing him. The smell of his skin right after sex, like salty honey. The way his pure white smile glints in the dark. The pressure of those long fingers leaving light bruises on my thighs when the pleasure gets to be too much.

I'm in full withdrawal from this man and can barely look at myself in the mirror for the shame of it, but I'll be damned if I'm the one who reaches out first. At the end of the day, J and I have not been acquainted for long and there are so many things we still need to learn about each other. It's my responsibility to teach him how to treat me. So, he can simmer in *my* silence while he figures out what he wants to do. I'm suffering in his absence but he doesn't have a clue; I plan to keep it that way.

Thankfully, keeping a watchful eye on Nikki at work keeps me distracted during the day, at least during the work week. The anxiety she causes made me cut way back on my usual caffeine intake, especially once I realized I kept checking the cup she always brings me for signs of tampering. I'm being paranoid, for sure. I know it. I highly doubt Nikki is even capable of doing something like that to someone.

I don't know…this whole thing with J and I on top of Nikki's previous advances on me…it's a lot. I've barely had an appetite lately with everything going on and have dropped a couple of pounds from the stress alone. One of the only benefits to the madness I've been dealing with.

If anyone at my job knew the suspicions I have about Nikki, they'd think I really was insane. Since she returned from her barely explained absence, she's been a model employee. Every aspect of her job she executes at near-perfection every day and I find I can't fault her for anything if I tried.

One single time, I do catch her looking at me with that same predatory gaze she employed during our exchange in the restroom, but she grins and it disappears so quickly I have to convince myself I saw it at all.

Nikki never tries any funny business. She barely even hugs me when she arrives or leaves anymore, anything beyond an arm thrown briefly over my shoulders. It takes a few work days before I feel like I can, but I finally force myself to relax in her presence until it feels natural again.

It doesn't take long. Nikki and I clicked immediately the first time we met, her sassy optimism meshing so well with my own. I fall right back into our usual rhythm at work with no resistance from her, and thank God for that. J and the stress he's causing is more than enough for one woman to handle without the fear of losing a good friend hanging over head.

My work day is mercifully uneventful for the first time in a while. As I pack up my purse to head home, I see a text notification pop up on my phone screen.

My heart lurches into a heavy thrum in my chest, my pulse and body temperature rising so fast I get lightheaded. I select the text with my heart in my suddenly dry throat.

It's shameful how crushing my disappointment is when I see it's Sherry reminding me that I promised to go to church with her during our conversation a few nights ago.

Still no J.

I squeeze my eyes shut with a weary sigh. I need to get a grip.

Damn, what if I've come to the conclusion that our break is temporary but J has already called it quits officially in his own mind? What if I'm being delusional?

"Hey, Boss."

My eyes open and I find Nikki smiling down at me from where she stands on the other side of my office desk.

I smile back despite my heavy heart. "You out of here, Nikki?"

"Yeah, but…I had a question for you." She wets her lips in a subtle way that makes my insides flutter a little and I cough into my fist to hide my discomfort. "I was getting ready to head to my kickboxing class. I notice you've been a little stressed out lately, so…you wanna come with?"

That question may as well be loaded with dynamite. Look at her — staring at me with those huge, innocent eyes. Nikki knows good and goddamn well I am lowkey terrified of being alone with her after everything that's gone down between us. Her query sounds to my ears like a sensual threat, but…maybe I can trust her to keep her hands to herself. And she has a good point about the potential for stress relief. Might do me some good to get in a good sweat session and release some of this tension in my body if I can't do the same for my mind.

Knowing how brazen Nikki has been within an office setting, hanging out with her in any capacity outside of these walls is taking a huge risk in more ways than one. Besides knowing J wouldn't like it, Nikki is the type of woman who will not be controlled by anyone or anything. There's no predicting what she might do.

I don't know. Could be a good thing if she manages to behave herself. And J can't exactly have an opinion on who I spend time with if the man doesn't want to have anything to do with me at the moment, anyway.

Nikki is poison.

J's words of warning flutter across my mind like a tattered flag in a breeze, but I let them pass me by. It's just a workout. And just *one*, not like I've signed up to meet with her at her gym every week on the regular. Not a big deal.

"Sure," I say, shouldering my bag and meeting her eyes like I have full faith in her intention of this being a completely innocent outing. I don't and can tell she doesn't either, but I can play along for now. "I don't have any workout clothes here, but I can pop into a store and buy something really quick…is your gym nearby? Like, am I meeting you there or are we walking together?"

"I always keep extra workout clothes in my locker, so you can borrow some." Nikki's smile stretches into a languorous grin. "And do you mind walking together? It's not far."

"Oh, no problem." I offer my fake nonchalance in the form of a shrug and follow Nikki out of the door, my heart banging hard inside my chest.

God, I need to calm down. It's just a stupid workout.

Having ditched our high heels for sneakers, Nikki and I merge seamlessly into the ever-present throng on the street. I still can't relax but Nikki doesn't seem to notice. She chats away about everything and nothing, cracking jokes about the coworkers of ours she doesn't like and waxing poetic about the ceviche she tasted at a new restaurant that blew her mind. Nice and normal. No talk that's even remotely sexual, which somehow gives me a sense of relief and disappointment in equal measure.

Nikki doesn't say anything that anyone could say was crazy or weird, in fact. Well, not really – Nikki often makes commentary that throws me for a loop and there are plenty of people who know her who'd say she was more than a little eccentric. But there's a very long road between crazy and dangerous.

The longer we talk about things that have nothing to do with our relationship and I begin to loosen up and laugh with her, J's warning about her feels more and more like blind jealousy. Of course, J would want me to stay away from Nikki. He's seen with his own eyes how I respond to her, and I know he could tell I'm attracted to her. Now that he is the one who has put our relationship in jeopardy, who is he to tell me to stay away from anyone? Honestly, I love him, but what a prick.

I can do whatever the hell I want.

The self-affirming thoughts put some pep in my step and Nikki and I arrive at her gym not long after.

My eyes go wide after we enter and I take in the place – all white, veined marble that covers the floor and partway up the walls. Very fancy. She makes enough to afford a membership here?

Nikki hands over her membership card to be swiped by the attendant at the front desk – made of the same marble – before handing me a blank swipe card presumably used for guests of the facility.

Nikki throws a wink at me over her shoulder. "Follow me."

I trail behind her down a sparkling clean hallway until we emerge from a side door into a large women's locker room. Nikki unlocks the padlock on her locker and tosses a bundle of fabric at me. "Those are for you," she says as I catch them against my chest. "Those are clean, of course. You never know when you might need them." Then she smiles and turns away.

Most of my brain knows there's a double meaning to her statement, but I'm too distracted by her body to focus on any of that. There's a couple of other ladies using this part of the locker room but Nikki strips down to literally nothing in full view of those milling around. I don't blame her; if my body was that perfect, I'd have unshakable confidence as well. Every part of her is so tight around the middle before blossoming into soft curves on the top and bottom…God, I'm staring. I look away before she can notice, changing into the borrowed t-shirt and pair of sweatpants with far more modesty than my coworker.

When I'm finished, Nikki claps her hands and bounces on her toes. "Ready? I think you're gonna love it. It completely changed my body and I have so much more energy."

"I think I am," I tell her. Nikki's already doing high kicks on our way out to the main workout floor, so she must be telling the truth about the energy boost. I definitely need some of that. Haven't really been able to sleep since J and I haven't been talking every night. He was usually the one who sent me straight to lullaby land, whether he was there with me in person or talking dirty to me in my ear on the phone.

I had initially been worried Nikki would let me embarrass myself in front of all these hyper-fit people lifting weights and going to town on punching bags around the gym, but I was totally wrong. I put out of my mind the stares from the few less fit men and women near the back of the gym – especially the older men. Nikki is so attentive I find myself blushing more than once as she walks me through her workout step by step. Especially when her hand lands innocently on the small of my back or gently stroke the undersides of my bare arms when she's showing me how to do a proper punch without injuring myself.

I can't lie – I love the attention. It feels amazing and my entire being soaks it up like a dried-up kitchen sponge. Nikki acts like there's no one in this gym except us. Her eyes never leave me. She laughs and encourages me when I mess up so I don't feel bad about it and give up, which I would if I were doing this my own. I work out, but not like this. Before I realize it, out little workout session starts to feel more like a… date. I end up having a good enough time with her to ignore the guilt that's starting to brew deep inside me.

An hour later, we walk back to the locker rooms flushed and sweaty. I giggle and gesture at the wisps of dark hair plastered to her forehead. "I don't think I've ever seen you sweat in real life."

Nikki throws her head back when she laughs, revealing her long, elegant throat. "I could say the same about you." A trickle of moisture works its way down from behind her ear and I blink at the insane urge that surges up in me to lean over and lick it off.

Nikki tosses me a miniature bottle of bodywash once we get back to her locker. "You can grab a clean towel by swiping your card at that little kiosk over there in the corner. The showers are on the other side of that same wall."

I turn to look where she's pointing and spot it. "Gotcha. I'll be back in a minute."

As soon as I'm alone again for the first time in hours, the sadness and guilt began to swirl together and weigh me down. Now I just want to get in and out of this shower and back home to wallow as soon as possible. Tonight is a night for takeout, ice cream, ugly pajamas, and trash TV.

The gym must have hit its evening lull because I find myself all alone in the shower, although with its multiple shower heads dangling from the ceiling in a long row, it's big enough for a whole party of people.

The spray is nice and warm when I step under it, spilling over my nakedness and down to the immaculately clean tile beneath my feet. I close my eyes and revel for a moment in the feeling of grime being rinsed away before I start to soap myself up from top to bottom. I'm thorough but move quickly. I don't want to leave Nikki waiting for me forever.

When I straighten after bending down to rinse off my feet, I almost scream at seeing Nikki directly in front of me, as if my thoughts have conjured her up. She's out of the spray but as naked as the day is long, licking her lips as she studies the swells of my breasts. I swear they grow heavier under her gaze.

I snap out of it and cross my arms over my chest to cover them and cross my legs to hide the rest of me. "Um, what are you doing?"

"I showered already," Nikki says, her openly hungry expression unchanging. "You were taking a while, so I figured you might need some help."

A nervous giggle escapes my throat. "I think I can manage, but thank you?"

She steps closer and my laughter turns a bit shrill. "Why are you acting like we've never seen each other naked before?"

"Entirely different context, Nikki. That matters." The shower is still warm but my entire body shivers.

Nikki takes two more steps, until her nose is inches away from mine, but she doesn't touch me. Her arms are loose and relaxed at her sides. Meanwhile, every muscle in my body is as taut as a drum. She's so close to my face my lips part on their own and I have to consciously clamp them together again.

"Nikki," I say, my voice suddenly as thin and wiry as an old woman's, "I'm still with J, if you forgot." More or less.

"So?" Nikki leans forward and braces one hand against the shower wall just behind my shoulder. Her nose trails over the shell of my ear and down my jawline. I just barely prevent a lustful whimper from escaping.

"So, this isn't exactly appropriate." I'm surprised I can still speak at all since out of nowhere I can't seem to breathe right.

Regardless, Nikki overpowers my already weak resistance with a single stroke of her thumb over my wet cheek. "Brooklyn, this is nothing the three of us haven't already done together." There's that carefree, tempting grin again. She might as well be Satan. "You can always tell him later what we're about to do now. In fact, I'm sure he'd appreciate hearing every detail." The tip of her soft, pink tongue traces the outline of my bottom lip and this time I can't help but moan. She smiles wider when she hears it and continues. "J loves you, right?" I nod helplessly, already under her spell. "Right. So, I know he'd be fine with you having a little fun with a friend you've known for years."

I'm pretty sure I'm not breathing at all now, because I try to speak and my chest heaves but nothing else happens beyond that. My brain has handed over all control to Nikki. Vaguely I'm aware anyone can walk in and see her pressing her entire naked body against mine in this shower and report us to security, but I can't make myself care.

My hands go up to brace myself against her narrow chest. I need to slow this down, to stop where I know this is going because there will be no coming back from it – this I know in my bones. But I still can't think straight when all I have are entire palmfuls of Nikki's ample tits. "I don't think he'll be as cool with this as you think," I tell her with the last remains of my good sense.

Nikki chuckles darkly. She knows she's already won. "I've known J longer than you have, babe. He'll understand," she says, then kisses me with her open mouth. I moan again at the exact moment our mouths meet, my legs parting unconsciously to keep my balance and creating just enough space for her to slide her entire hand between my legs and palm my pussy. Which is so slick with my arousal my face practically bursts into flames from embarrassment, but I can't do anything but let her continue to kiss me. Because I need it. I need to feel something good to make me forget about everything else.

She giggles at my responding growl into her mouth. "You're so fucking wet. That has nothing to do with the shower." While I watch her, panting, Nikki stares into my heavy-lidded eyes and licks the entire length of her palm, moaning with pleasure at the flavor she discovers. "God, I missed that," she says, and the way she falls to her knees before me makes me believe every word.

Her hands press me back against the wall, more forcefully than I can ever remember her being at the BDSM club. She shoves my legs further apart with her shoulders and attaches her mouth to my sex like she was ready to feed and I was keeping her alive. Her soft mouth probes the lips there, gentle at first and then more urgently as she reaches underneath me to knead my ass cheeks.

Jesus. It so fucking good my entire body feels like it's vibrating, like I'm lifting off to another plane of existence. I never expected being alone with her like this would feel so intense, but my knees are already trembling.

Nikki moans into my folds almost as much as I do into the hands I've clamped over my mouth to keep myself quiet, writhing in her hold as her tongue moves over and around my mound like she is possessed. Oh, fuck. Oh, *fuck.*

Without pausing, Nikki pushes into me one finger, then two. Then *three.* I've had more experiences with this than I can count at this point in my life, but I still have to slap both hands against the wall behind me to brace myself and keep from toppling over onto her head.

Four fingers in and I'm almost sobbing, my hips jerking against her in time to Nikki's thrusts all own their own. She moans when I moan, yelps when I yelp. As if her fingers inside me and her tongue massaging my clit have given her a direct link to my soul.

"Look at me."

I can barely see past the stars clouding my vision, but I do as Nikki commands. I almost erupt on the spot when I see her entire hand except for her thumb is wedged between my pelvic bones, only half of it visible. Her face looks beautiful and demented when Nikki looks up at me again. "I want you to come so hard I can't feel my fingers."

I don't even think that's a tall order. The orgasm that had been glinting like gold on the horizon of my mind is now right in front of me, beckoning me off the edge into an abyss I've never known.

"I'll see what I can do," I barely manage to say and Nikki goes back to doing what she apparently does best. My clit gets flicked, rubbed, sucked. My depths are probed and stroked. My asshole is tended to with a tenderness that makes me literally want to scream my head off in this public venue, but I manage to refrain because I still don't want to get arrested. Just barely.

Then Nikki somehow manages to curl all four of her fingers at once, tapping on the inside of my walls. My smooth inner muscles finally do clamp down on her fingers and it feels like bombs goes off in every cell, dropping open my mouth in a silent scream that wracks my body.

Nikki had a point, though – I'm not sure I'm alive right now, but if I do survive this, I promise I will tell J everything that happened here today.

I *will.*

Eight

I thought the aftermath of my post-workout activities with Nikki in the very public gym shower would be fraught with tension and weirdness. I just knew she would be super clingy as soon as we left. I half expected her to be calling me seconds after we parted ways to go home, the sun slipping away beyond the New York skyline.

In fact, it turned out to be quite the opposite. Nikki kissed me on the cheek after a close hug, during which she held on to me like she was afraid I'd shatter in her thin, muscular arms. Then she left me standing there for a moment, still stunned after everything that happened between us, and I didn't see or hear from her again until work the next morning. She didn't push up on me or press me. She didn't take liberties and assume she now had a certain access to my life because she knew the flavor of my womanhood. I had my life and she had hers. We would intermingle them when we both saw fit, not when one of us decided to be ready to do that for the other and force the issue.

Nikki's usual attentiveness at work hasn't changed, but now it's charged with a protectiveness and tenderness that was definitely absent before we were intimate together without J for the first time. If I didn't know better, I'd say she's treating me like a really good boyfriend – anticipating my every need and leaving sweet notes of encouragement and humor around my office.

At first, it makes me uncomfortable because the guilt that sneaked up on me after the last echoes of my orgasm dissipated consumed me immediately and I couldn't think of anything else. But she is so sweet to me and so consistent about it, I can't help but start to relax into it.

Nikki is poison and all that foolishness. Yeah, right. Nikki, though I still can't believe it, is more of a gentleman than J is in many ways when it comes to how to properly treat a woman. I may have known Nikki longer than I have J, but I knew about her parents and family life and where she went to school within weeks of meeting her – things that are still murky and dark when it comes to J. He could actually take a lesson or two from her when it comes to openness and honesty. And respecting the boundaries of the person you claim to care about in a relationship.

Is that what this was growing into with Nikki?

I'm not ready for that with her, that much I do know. But what's the harm in enjoying the attentions of someone who is clearly as into me as I am into them? Like she told me, if J is as open as he claims to be, he wouldn't see my being with Nikki from time to time as cheating if I don't hide it from him, and I don't plan to. Maybe the guilt still tugging at the edge of my consciousness is just societal conditioning and would work itself out. I hope so, anyway. At some point the nausea would have to go away, right?

Honestly, it's fine. J isn't worried about me right now, so I shouldn't be worried about him. Memories of all the many moments we've shared will eventually stop making my stomach drop whenever they cross my mind. Since he's decided he needs a break, I'll let him have it and be grown enough to entertain an adult conversation when he decides to come back around. And it will then be *my* decision if we continue.

If he asked me today if I still wanted to be with him after what just happened with Nikki…I don't know what I would tell him. That's an uneasy space to be in.

I don't share any of my misgivings with Nikki. The emotions are too heavy and frankly, I'm tired of suffocating under their weight. I just want to feel free and easy. I don't want to continue obsessing over the hows and whys of my relationship with J when right now there aren't any answers for me to obtain.

I'm tired of thinking about this shit.

So, I keep things light with Nikki, which turns out to be perfect timing for that decision. The heads of the TV station where I work have decided to completely revamp the programming next year based on all the viewership data gathered over the past twelve months. That means at least a full week of all the producers and their staff crunching numbers and scrambling for ideas in think tanks for new shows for every single time slot. It has been a long time since there's been sweeping changes at the station with so large a scope, but it means most of us will be here in our offices more than we are home for the next few long, exhausting days.

More than once, I just want to kiss Nikki full on the mouth in gratitude alone. She powers through all the work we have to do at my side without faltering, even though I know she's as tired as I am. She keeps protein snacks and caffeine at the ready for when my energy levels tank out and makes time and space for me to have power naps undisturbed between the back-to-back producer planning meetings we have during this time. I've never had to go looking for data or spreadsheets because she always has exactly what I need in my hands when I need it, every time. Nikki even started giving me shoulder massages toward the end of hell week – she turned out to be an amazing amateur masseuse on top of everything else – when my muscles are so tight from all the stress and deadlines I can barely move normally. Always with a smile on her face, even when I'm grouchy because I'm completely spent and my blood sugar is too low for me to be chipper and upbeat any longer.

Not once does Nikki hint that she wants sex from me again. She calls me after work but it's only to check in and shoot the bull long enough for both of us to blow off steam. At work she's just kind and attentive, almost loving without the sexuality. So much so that when Friday hits and things have gone so well due to our combined level of commitment that we end up not having to work on Saturday, it's me that locks my office door and gives her soft lips a grateful kiss.

Is this what an official relationship with Nikki might look like? Mutual respect, adoration and mind-blowing sex?

Jesus, a real relationship with a woman would have been inconceivable to me a year ago. A relationship with my long-time assistant at work would have had me questioning my own sanity.

Now, though? I don't know. The idea is growing on me, but I don't tell Nikki that when she leans back, dazed from the clearly unexpected kiss. Truthfully, I didn't expect to be the one initiating the kissing.

Her voice is dreamy and soft. "What was that for?"

My smile is genuine. "I just appreciate you. More than you know. You've been amazing this week and I know it's been rough for both of us, so thank you."

"You make it easy," she says, aiming her suddenly shy smile down at her knees before she reaches for my hand. I don't feel the urge to pull away when she laces her fingers through mine on her lap. My mother would probably have a heart attack if I brought Nikki home to meet her –

I'm getting ahead of myself. Definitely not in love nor trying to plan a future with Nikki right now, I'm just…enjoying her company and trying not to think about J so much. Nothing wrong with that.

Nikki has such a warm, fun and sexy energy that with all the negativity plaguing my mind right now, I can't get enough of it.

There's been something on my mind all day and I'm scared to put the question out there, but it's now or never. "Hey, do you have anything planned tomorrow?" I'm surprised my voice doesn't tremble from my nervousness.

Nikki's eyes get wide. "No, why? What's up?"

"Well, there's this street fair happening in my neighborhood this weekend and…I was wondering if you might wanna go. You know, with me." The words are hanging in the air and yeah, I just asked Nikki out on a date. While my boyfriend is on ice. Totally normal.

"Hell, yeah!" Nikki says, pulling a laugh from me. "That sounds like fun. I'd love to."

"Good." I squeeze her hand, feeling more buoyant and optimistic than I have in what seems like months. It's been a long while since I looked forward to something this much. That has to mean something. "Can't wait."

I'm still more than a little tired the next morning, but at least it's because I was too excited to sleep rather than my tossing and turning in turmoil because of the limbo I still exist in with J. I feel like a teenager getting ready to go on a date, and the excitement and sense of possibility push me out of bed before the sun to get ready.

I texted Nikki the address last night and told her I'd meet her at the street fair early this afternoon. I have hours before then to prepare so I take my time primping to make sure I look and smell – and feel – extra delectable. I don't know what will happen between Nikki and I there or afterward, but I want to be ready for anything.

Before I get in the shower, I grab my phone to check my messages purely out of habit. Right on cue, my heart sinks when I don't see evidence of any contact attempts from J and I heave a sigh as I step under the spray. I just don't understand it. I had been prepared for the sizzling anger at his dismissal of my feelings that usually hits me with any reminder of him, but it doesn't come this time. Now, it feels like an empty pit has opened in my stomach, like how I imagine it would feel if I jumped off the top of a building with nothing to catch my fall.

J and I had had an argument. He walked off and left me alone, rejection of the highest order. Fine, all that happened, but now I see my emotional reaction to it within myself may have been a little overblown. Couples fight all the time. Even break up just as often. That doesn't mean they never come together again.

It just doesn't seem like him to cut off all communication like that overnight with no explanation or closure. Something about it just doesn't feel right.

What if something had happened to him?

Nah. I roll my eyes at myself and get out to towel off. We might live in New York City but the odds of a man of J's age and physique being murdered or kidnapped are slim to none. He's always had a don't-fuck-with-me kind of air about him. He can handle himself.

J isn't speaking to me *simply because he doesn't want to.* Probably to punish me. Which may or may not be working.

I need to let things be what they are for now. Everything will work out the way they're supposed to. Today is going to be great. I can feel it. Besides, Nikki deserves my attention and I plan on lavishing her with it this afternoon. It's the least I can do for everything she's done for me.

It's warmer than I expect on my walk to meet Nikki. I can already smell the street fair from here, still blocks away. The air is heavy with fragrant cut flowers and spices from exotic countries around the world, the delectable scents of seasoned meats cooking over open flames. I'm glad I was too jittery to eat breakfast early this morning, because that food smells so good there's no way I'm not partaking. Sundress and lipstick be damned, I'm not too cute to stuff my face.

I find Nikki already waiting for me at the entrance of the fair, an entire street cordoned off and lined on either side with canvas booths selling any and everything. Her face lights up when she sees me, but for a moment my vision is filled with her tight, petite curves stuffed into a matching tube top and mini skirt made up in leather the color of merlot.

"Hi," I say, leaning in to wrap my arms around her in a hug. Nikki embraces me but captures my mouth in a heated kiss.

The passion it contains hits me like a freight train at full speed and I physically falter, stumbling back a step before I can steady myself. Everything about it is soft and tender and she smells like cinnamon and vanilla…it overwhelms me and I catch myself just before I moan aloud and embarrass myself in front of all these people around us.

"Hello," Nikki says after she pulls away, then gives an adorably shy laugh that lets me know she was just as affected by the kiss she's just laid on me. A few seconds later, I'm still seeing stars.

"I'd say you're pretty happy to see me." I rub the back of my neck and glance around instead of looking into Nikki's eyes. This is way too intense.

"I am. And you were taking forever."

I make a face. "Excuse me? You're acting like I was late."

"I guess it just felt like forever," Nikki says with a grin, then slips her hand into mine. "Let's go – I'm ready to eat."

The fair isn't large so I expected Nikki and I to spend an hour there together max before we'd need to find something else to do. We end up having such a good time just talking and enjoying each other's company, we spend hours just wandering up and down the aisle examining the wares. An older gentleman in the crowd seems to take an interest in watching us as we hold hands. We must look cute together. We munch on kettle corn and sausage on sticks. Try on jewelry and hats. Ride the little train on wheels that winds through the whole affair slower than we could walk – both of us laughing our heads off about how ridiculous we look on this slow-ass kiddie ride. But that's most of the fun.

I *feel* like a kid again, carefree and joyful. I had no idea how much I've missed this. It's giving me life right now.

The train heads back to where it picked us up. Giddy, I lean into Nikki's shoulder and give her a sidelong look. "So, tell me: when was the last time you did something like this?"

She laughs, choking briefly on her mouthful of the saltwater taffy she's been stuffing into her mouth for the last few minutes from our shared plastic candy sack. She's so dramatic in her recovery it makes me burst out laughing as well.

"I was probably in high school or something," she finally manages to say.

"Really?" I would have expected her to be going out or doing something fun all the time.

Her eyebrows raise. "Why is that surprising?"

"I don't know. You just seem like the type to go out every weekend."

Nikki's eyes flash dangerously, her top teeth catching on her full bottom lip and making her look a little feral. "I do go out a lot, but I tend to get into…other things."

A flash of heat pulses through me as she stares back at me. I'll just bet she does.

Evening arrives in a cool breeze and a wash of pinkish orange across the sky. Every so often I'll catch a shy glance from Nikki out of the corner of my eye as we keep a leisurely pace walking back to the entrance of the street fair. I'm not sure what it is about this day, but being here with her just feels right, even with things with J still up in the air.

And speaking of air, I feel a little bit like I'm floating. Not sure what that means, but I know I don't want this effervescent feeling to evaporate into nothing.

Nikki and I pause near the same spot where I found her waiting hours ago, both clinging to each other's hands like we don't want to let go.

I look at Nikki. She looks at me, then smiles like she already knows what I'm going to say before I open my mouth.

She can probably feel the heat rolling off me at the thought of peeling that tiny skirt down her long legs.

The chemistry between us crackles like a live wire. I can barely think straight.

Anyway…we both know where this is going tonight.

I keep it short and to the point. "You want to come over?"

Nikki doesn't say anything. Her answer is clear when she grins and squeezes my hand, looking up at me expectantly to lead the way back to my apartment.

My door closes and Nikki and I are on each other in an instant – hands roaming then grabbing with increasing urgency, exploring with lips and tongue and teeth. My skin is singing. An inferno blazes through my veins and I'm so wet I know I've soaked right through my panties.

Nikki reaches under my sundress and rips the moist fabric off me with surprising strength, replacing them with the palm of her hand like she did in the gym shower – and god*damn,* I had no idea how good that particular move could feel with her soft, slender hand. A woman's touch feels so different down there than that of man. This is the first time I've really explored it, and I want so much more.

I can't hear much past the pounding in my own ears, but I can see Nikki's open and panting mouth, the wanton lust on her face a perfect reflection of everything I'm feeling. She wants this as much as I do. That's such a freeing moment to exist in with another person, especially one as gorgeous as Nikki.

I've never specifically wanted to fuck a woman's brains out before, but here I am.

I grab her hands and yank her into my bedroom without another thought.

We don't take our time. Fabric goes flying as we practically tear each other's clothes off in the effort to feed our fingers bare skin as quickly as possible. As soon as we are both naked, my hands slide from her narrow shoulders and over the swells of her breasts not far below, down to the tiniest waist imaginable. When I grip her there, my fingertips almost meet in the small of her back.

She leans forward and flicks the tip of her tongue at my lips like a coiling serpent ready to strike.

I shove her hard enough for her to lose her balance and fall against my mattress. Nikki lands on her back and parts her thighs with a giggle, like she had had every intention of ending up there, just like this.

Crawling onto the bed, I dive face-first between her legs. The second that sweet, tangy flavor hits my tongue I wonder how I ever lived without it. Another aspect of my life that previously only existed in monochrome bursts into full color. I treat Nikki to the same technique she used on me in the shower and she writhes beneath me and howls, back arched and nails digging into my arms as she takes her pleasure from my mouth and tongue and fingers.

She's so wet. She's so wet and hot and soft and I couldn't make myself stop tasting her if the room was on fire. I keep moving until Nikki's breathing gets short and choppy. A moment later, her body shudders and she unleashes a high-pitched squeal in the throes of her climax that sounds like music to me.

Nikki wastes no time recovering, pulling me forward and down and crawling down my body until she's sitting on my face and she's burying hers in my pussy. We linger in this position for a long time, time grinding to a halt as we feed each other ecstasy.

I'm riding out yet another orgasm when I'm stunned into silence as Nikki flips around onto her knees, grabs the backs of mine and pushes my legs up until I'm spread-eagled on the mattress.

She licks her lips as she stares down at my center, glossy and slick from everything we've been doing so far. Her eyes flick up to look at me. "You ever done this before?"

What did she mean? Have sex with a woman? My brain is sluggish due to the constant flood of feel-good neurochemicals, so my IQ has to be a least twenty points lower than normal right now. "Huh? You'll have to be more specif – *oh, God!*"

Nikki laughs, her grip tightening painfully on my ankles, and keeps grinding her pussy directly on mine, aggressively bucking her hips as if she were wearing a strap-on. Earlier, I had had half a mind to grab the one dildo I kept in the back of my nightstand drawer for emergencies but forgot about it as soon as I remembered it. This feels so good, penetration would be extraneous.

I – I think my overstimulated brain just combusted. She pins me down and I am completely at her mercy, the moans in my throat growing in intensity until I'm so loud I'm sure my neighbors can hear.

I've never felt anything like it. She's as bald down below as I am and so slick and hot against me, I'm about to lose my fucking mind. Our sounds fill the air, bouncing off the walls, the ceiling. Nikki pauses for a moment to readjust her stance so she's balancing herself on her heels while holding onto my hips. I'm already so close to coming again, each one of my breaths comes out sounding like a trembling wheeze as I try to keep it together.

For what feels like the hundredth time this evening, my mind is blown: Nikki's hands slide inward, and she spreads my lips with her fingers, baring the swollen nub of my clit that is more plump than I've ever seen it. Then she proceeds to align her body so her clit is touching mine.

I yelp and she hasn't even moved yet, but I don't have to wait long. Nikki starts jerking her hips like she's riding a bucking bronco, both our pussies sliding against the wetness that we're making together. Jesus fucking Christ…it's too much. It's way too much. Seconds later, I'm screaming into another climax and Nikki follows right behind me, grunting in time to her thrusts. Then I realize I can feel her muscles contracting against my opening and come again before the initial one is completely over.

That was…I thought everything J and I have done was intense, but… this? This was next level. For a full minute or so, I couldn't remember my name or who I was.

We take a long time catching our breath. At some point, Nikki rights herself in the bed and curls up against my side amidst the rumpled sheets. She lays her head on my shoulder. My eyes still closed; I hum with contented pleasure as she toys with one of my nipples.

"I think I'm falling in love with you, Brooklyn."

My eyes shoot open and I'm pretty sure my heart just stopped.

Worst. Case. Scenario.

Nine

Three fucking weeks.

Well, twenty-four days, if I'm being entirely accurate. And I know I am, because I've felt the tick of every single second of those days go by like a gong in my gut, leaving me off-kilter and sick to my stomach.

Goddammit…it was so much easier to feel like J did in fact break up with me during our argument at my mom's house and just didn't officially call it quits because he was a coward. That he wasn't the man I thought he was and needed him to be. It was easier to be pissed off.

But it's been too long. This isn't like him. The emotional chasm I put between us that night on the sidewalk has grown too wide and I'm starting to feel like it'll be too big a gap to bridge if I don't do something. Or say something.

Anything.

In reality, I don't want to just let him go.

Where's the rage and righteous indignation when I need it? It's like J's lack of contact hit the three-week mark and *poof* – all my heated emotion about the matter disappeared in a puff of smoke. Now all I feel is a gnawing, debilitating worry that makes me want to crawl out of my skin to be rid of it.

More than once I dreamed J had been killed in grievous fashion and woke up sobbing like I'd just come back from his funeral, but I pushed the very concept into the depths of my mind the second I had dried my eyes and gotten myself together. No point in thinking like that – J's fine. He's just being an asshole by not reaching out when he *knows* he was the one in the wrong.

The thought of contacting him first feels like a hot poker twisting my intestines. My pride is making it extremely difficult to do so, no matter how much the rest of me wants to.

Especially because I know *something* is wrong beyond the physical. I can feel it. Now, whether or not that something in J's world is the hot snatch of another woman and him being truly done with me, I have no idea.

Regardless, it's all I can think about, no matter how hard I try to occupy my mind with any and everything else. I can barely concentrate at work. I've been a space cadet at family dinner, unable to keep up with the conversation going on around me without asking for things to be repeated again and again. More than one member of my church congregation has surreptitiously let me know that they are praying for me, saying I am clearly going through something because the devil is busy.

Ain't that the truth. But how much of these trials and tribulations I'm experiencing are caused by J, and how much of it am I doing to myself?

I don't know and right now, I don't care. I just know I am currently too psychologically uncomfortable to sleep or eat normally – I haven't slept more than a couple of hours at a time or eaten three square meals in weeks. Hence the current knock on my door at nearly midnight.

I tip the delivery driver with a shameful smile and wave him off before scurrying back inside my apartment with my prize: a box of oversized sugar cookies the size of my face.

This may or may not be the third time I've ordered from this place since the last time J and I spoke. To be fair, I wasn't expecting to have gone this long without talking to my own boyfriend to necessitate the consumption of emergency sweets, but it is what it is. Desperate measures, and all that. At least I've been doubling up on my sessions at the gym; it would definitely be a bad look to put on twenty pounds when J and I get back together. *If* we get back together.

The cookies are still *warm.* They smell so good my eyes roll back in my head for a moment, and I cross my legs under my chenille blanket on the couch and tuck into them immediately, watching whatever was playing on the TV but registering nothing. It takes all of twenty seconds for my eyes to wander down to my cell phone on the coffee table next to the cookie box. The screen is dark and silent as the grave.

I sigh heavily and stuff the last bite of my first cookie into my mouth, chewing and glaring at the phone. I can't even say I'm still angry at J now. Annoyed? Yes. Bereft? Absolutely.

I have to stop doing this to myself. All I need to do is call him and this unsettling feeling of being suspended in limbo would instantly go away. Even if J is angry or nonchalant – I don't care. I…I just want to hear his voice.

Grabbing my phone like a lifeline, I wake it up and ignore the multiple text messages I've received today from Nikki – I don't have the mental energy to deal with any of that. It's taking all I have to muster up the courage to dial up J's number. My stomach drops when I realize it's been so long since I've talked to him on the phone that I have to scroll through my recent calls to see his number.

My hands tremble as I tap the speaker button and the line trills. I can't breathe, but I have to follow through. I can't keep living like this.

Ring. Ring. Ring.

Ring.

His voicemail comes on, his voice smooth as melted butter. It gives me a full-body shudder to hear it but even as I take in a breath to leave a message, I chicken out and hang up instead.

I don't trust my voice not to tremble. Calling him in the first place is already doing a number on my pride as a woman; I don't want to add insult to injury by doing so from a clear place of weakness.

But the tension that lingers in the silence after I hang up just ramps up even higher, and before I know it, I'm calling right back.

Voicemail again.

So, I hang up…again.

Gnawing on my lip, I pull up our text thread and avoid reading through the most recent ones and triggering myself. I type "*hey*" and hit send before I can talk myself out of it.

Minutes go by that feel like hours. No response.

Like some desperate fool, I text "hello?" and wait once more.

I squint down at the phone screen. Damn, did it go through at all? But it says both texts were delivered…*shit*.

When I sigh this time, my chest is so tight it comes out like a wheeze. My eyes dance wildly around my apartment for help, but of course, there's no one here but me.

I run a hand through my wild curls. Haven't bothered to do more than put it in a high bun in forever, but my mind is far too preoccupied to bother with such mundane things as top-tier personal grooming when I'm busy losing my mind.

I can't even call someone in his family to check on J's welfare because I don't know who the fuck they are, let alone have their personal numbers saved in my phone. J has never sat down and given me the who's who of his relatives and friends. To this day I'm in the dark, and that's our main problem – he has taken full access to my life without reciprocation. That hasn't gone away despite his sudden absence.

Our issues aside, I need to be thinking about solutions instead of more problems.

I could always go over to his place. Try to track down some family members on social media. Or call the police for a wellness check. All of those options make me wring my hands. The last thing I want to do is make the worst-case scenario real.

I take a deep breath. No, reaching out is enough. He'll be able to see that he's been on my mind. J was always good at reading between the lines.

The phone lights up in my hands, making my heart lurch so hard I nearly drop it. A text comes through – from Nikki.

My entire body sags with disappointment. Not the person I want to hear from right now, but that's okay. I just hope she's not coming at me with some bullshit because I can't handle that right now. My nerves are too frayed as it is.

When I open my text thread with her, I just find a coffee emoji and a question mark – morning plans for work, I presume, since I brought the fancy coffee drinks last time. My shoulders manage to relax for the moment.

I have zero time to think about work but I text her back a thumbs up, and that's it. Nothing more than that. I don't want to give Nikki the wrong idea.

I'm still not sure exactly what I said to her after her love confession the night we had sex, but I managed to weasel my way out of the awkward situation by kissing her passionately and changing the subject to what we were eating for dinner. I didn't bring it up again after that and neither did she.

Honestly, I was a little afraid of how she would react if I had to tell her I didn't feel the same way. I love her as a friend and I absolutely care for her as a lover, but I didn't know for sure it wasn't romantic love I felt until she put it out there like that when I was least expecting it. I'm just glad she hasn't pushed for a response since then. But something tells me it's not over.

A few moments later, Nikki's responding text came through – a heart eyes emoji – and I let it drop and don't text back, not wanting to tempt fate. I'd see her in a few hours anyway.

I down another cookie while I wait for a response to my text to J with my heart in my throat, literally twiddling my thumbs as I stare at the screen and will it to light up. Nothing else happens and I toss the remaining half of my cookie aside with disgust.

At least Nikki doesn't seem to be as clingy as she had been after our night together. It was beyond intense for me sexually, but her declaration immediately afterward made it clear she was experiencing something that I just…wasn't. Even if I wanted to. And I did.

I feel bad about it. Nikki wasn't overbearing or anything like I expected her to be, but I heard from her multiple times a day via a call or text and it was just…too much. I imagine anyone would want a new lover's attention like that – a normal person, at least. After our mind-blowing night – and it really was just that – I just couldn't seem to muster up the emotional energy for her anymore, try as I might. Once the orgasmic afterglow faded, all I could think about was J. It was like starving and sitting down to eat an entire chocolate cake by yourself instead of a nourishing meal – yeah, it's delicious, but now you feel sick as hell and never want chocolate again.

Nikki is my friend and has been for years. I think I was just fooling myself thinking we could ever be more than that. And I'm going to have to tell her.

My stomach twists into an even tighter knot. That's not a conversation I'm looking forward to having, but that's a problem for another day.

Of course, tonight is no different than the last few of weeks in my life – I hardly sleep at all. I lie on my side with my knees tucked against my chest, staring at the glowing red numbers on the digital clock on my nightstand and counting my blinks between each minute that passes. As time crawls toward the early hours of morning, my bed has never felt so empty. Intimacy with Nikki between my sheets was a lovely distraction but holding her felt like some kind of consolation no matter how much I cared about her.

It is J's soothing, solid warmth curled around me from behind that I miss, one of his long, heavy legs thrown over my hip so I don't wander away from him in my sleep. I always loved that.

I'm still thinking about it by the time I make it to work, shoulders sagging from the fruitless watch over my phone. Even after sending a few more texts and calling, J still hasn't answered.

Nikki, on the other hand, has texted at least three times since I got up this morning. As bad as I felt about it, I ignored them all. Hopefully, she can stay business-minded today once she gets here. I don't have the emotional bandwidth for anything else.

I ease into my morning routine, stopping by the offices of each of my fellow producers for a quick chat I hope can boost my mood a bit. One of the guys tells some ridiculous joke that actually makes me laugh, so it works, but only for a little while. By the time I'm back in my own office and sitting behind my desk, the sadness and anxiety settle back over me like a thick, itchy blanket.

I don't want to think about anything but work, so I dive head-first into the paperwork I need to finish that Nikki had left stacked neatly on my desk in their respective manila envelopes before she left work last Friday. Mercifully, I get caught up in the process and don't realize a couple of hours have gone by until I look at the clock.

Out of habit, my eyes flit to where my coffee cup would normally be. It's not there. Because *Nikki* isn't here.

It's been hours…where the hell is she?

Now I *do* drag out my phone and dial her up…and she doesn't answer. A frown settles in when I get her voicemail.

"Um, hey Nikki…this is Brooklyn, of course. Where are you?" I say, up from my chair and pacing as I leave the message. "Let me know if you're still coming in, okay? I'm starting to get a little worried."

I hang up, already gnawing my lip when it registers how anxious I sounded to my own ears. I don't need another person I care about disappearing from my life with little to no explanation. But I'm not going to allow myself to catastrophize Nikki's situation as well. Regardless, this no-show behavior is starting to become habitual and I am not a fan. Her text last night made it seem like she had every intention of coming to work like normal, coffee in hand for both of us.

What did Nikki text me this morning, anyway? I saw the notifications but I hadn't taken the time to actually read them.

I do so now, my anxiety spiking once again via bunched shoulders as I scroll through our text thread. The ones she sent this morning were random memes that didn't make a ton of sense, but nothing about not coming in today. No missed calls from her, either.

A knock on my office door raises my head, interrupting my thoughts. I smile when I see the assistant for one of the newer producers. "Oh – hey, James." He looks ultra-sharp in his baby blue suit. He's supremely stylish, outdressing me these last few weeks. Not that it would have been difficult with how I've been looking lately. "What's up?"

"There's a guy at the front desk asking for Nikki, but I haven't seen her anywhere." His lips purse and he suddenly looks as irritable as I feel. "Have you?"

"No. I was just texting her to see where she is, but I haven't heard back yet."

Wonder who that could be…in all the years Nikki and I have worked together, I can't recall her getting any visitors here at the office. Not even a random boyfriend – or girlfriend – stopping by to drop off flowers or whisk her off to a fancy lunch.

James blinks at me impatiently, holding on to the edge of my door like he's prepared to flee as soon as I give the word. "Brooklyn, did you want to…"

"Yeah, sorry – I'll go talk to him."

"Thanks." James's smile is tight and brief before he disappears from view.

Putting my phone down, I straighten my suit skirt and blouse, smooth my hair, then go to meet the mysterious visitor at the front desk.

The receptionist usually goes to lunch early, so her chair is empty when I approach the wide front desk in the lobby to our floor. I spot the guy James told me about and just feel more confused. He's on the shorter side – probably an inch or two shorter than I am, I don't consider myself a tall woman. Standing a couple of paces away from the desk, his pudgy hands are folded before him as he stares out of the window. The only hair on his head is a brown, patchy ring of tight curls that stretches from the back of one ear to the other and is peppered with gray. His suit somehow manages to be the color of his hair, making him look washed out and tired.

Was Nikki getting served a lawsuit or something? I can't imagine how she would even be acquainted with a man like this well enough for him to know where she worked and be so bold as to come up here looking for her. Not that he's necessarily unattractive – when he turns to face me, his watery eyes are the color of honey and his long dimples flash when he offers a smile that looks unnecessarily grim.

I smile back, doing my best to ignore the dread yanking at the pit of my stomach. "Can I help you? I believe you were looking for my assistant, Nikki."

The man's eyes glaze over at the mention of her name. "Uh, yes." When he speaks, I can hear the gravel in his voice as if he hadn't spoken in years. His eyes wander around the office for so long, I wonder if he's lost his train of thought.

"Sir? Are...you a relative? She's not here...did you want to leave a message?"

The hairs on my arms and back of my neck stand straight up as the guy's eyes continue to wander, as if I wasn't standing right in front of him. He seems a billion miles away. He doesn't seem dangerous, not with his sloped shoulders and puppy-dog demeanor, but I am two seconds from calling security if he doesn't answer me or leave.

I thought he may have been her father at first. Nikki had told me in the past that she didn't have the best relationship with him. Age-wise he fits the part, but something about him is just...off. It's starting to make me more than a little uncomfortable.

His eyes finally find mine again and I raise my eyebrows. "You said she's not here?"

"No, she's not." He just stares at me. "Sir, if you – "

"Thank you," he says, then does an about-face and heads straight for the exit via the bank of elevators.

What the hell was that? I stare after him, keeping an eye out until the elevators close and he finally disappears.

I sigh wearily, looking around only to find that the lobby is virtually empty today and no one saw that strangeness but me.

Shaking my head at myself, I wait around for a few minutes to see if the man decides to come back, but he doesn't. I stay until the receptionist comes back and then I return down the hall to my office.

My anxiety is so high now my stomach is actually fluttering. I snatch my phone off my desk and almost throw it across the room when I don't see a text or a missed call from *anyone*. Still no Nikki. Or J.

I'm running on autopilot the rest of the day, but I suppose the only difference between today and the past few weeks is that now a feeling too close to fear is creeping up and down my spine and raising goosebumps all over my body. I manage to make it through my duties for the day without Nikki's help – she never shows up or reaches out – with seemingly only half my brain activated. Thank God for the muscle memory and routine that is my saving grace. That and the fact that we aren't as busy today as I had expected to be.

Before I know it, it's the end of the day and time to go home. I gather up my things. Swallow hard. Pull out my phone that I've successfully ignored the existence of all afternoon.

My hand trembles when I dial Nikki's number and wait for it to ring. It does, again and again, then goes to voicemail.

I hang up and feel inexplicably sick to my stomach.

Something's wrong. Very wrong. I don't know what it is or how I know, but I do.

My first thought is to call my mother, but she's teaching right now and won't be available. I can't call the police because I literally have nothing to tell them. I don't want to get either of my siblings involved in this, so that's not even an option.

So, I take a deep breath and send yet another text to Nikki:

Hey, is everything okay?

I gasp when I get a response a few seconds later.

No.

God, was she sick or hurt? Why wouldn't she just answer the phone?

I know you called. Can't talk right now.

My eyes take in the message. Apparently, Nikki is a mind reader now. Whatever. If this is the only way she can communicate at the moment, I'll take it for now. I quickly tap out a message.

What's wrong?

I think I stop breathing while I wait for Nikki to text back this time.

I love you but you're pulling away. I can feel it.

My entire body is shaking now as if the temperature in my office has plunged fifty degrees. I can barely get my fingers to cooperate to respond to her.

What are you talking about?

I know, of course. Nikki is no idiot. That's exactly what I've been doing – pulling away. Maintaining distance and space to make the decisions I need to make for my life. And that's not a crime, but I need to make sure she and I see it the same way. Something tells me she doesn't.
Nikki leaves no doubt when she responds.

J is in the way, Brooklyn. You don't see it but I do. So, it's clear I'll need to force you to make a choice.

A choice? What choice? I'm trying too hard to stay calm and keep my racing heart from bursting out of my chest, but I'm not doing very well.

I haven't even worked out in my mind what to say to her when Nikki sends another text and my heart drops heavily into my pelvis like a stone.

If you ever want to see J again, come to his apartment right now. And come alone.

Ten

If you ever want to see J again, come to his apartment right now. And come alone.

I had unconsciously committed Nikki's text to memory in just a few seconds but I read it again and again and again anyway. I can't stop myself. I can't believe what I'm reading. I don't trust my eyes to tell me the truth, even though I'm staring right at it on my phone screen.

I don't know how long I've been pacing the floor in my office, but I can't seem to stop doing that either. I have to do something with this pent-up panic trapped inside my body so I can think like a rational human being.

Nikki's text is clearly a threat. But what kind? If I show up over there, is she gonna pop up with a wife and kids that he's been hiding from me or something? Because surely this isn't an actual threat of bodily harm…

How – why –

Ugh. I huff out a frustrated breath and keep pacing, phone in hand. I haven't responded because I am in new territory now. Hell, I'm in the fucking Twilight Zone. My assistant and lover are now threatening me with "choices" and using my estranged boyfriend as some kind of bargaining chip. And for what? What is she hoping to achieve by sending messages like this?

I pause my long strides long enough to notice how dark it has gotten since I logged off of my work computer for the day. God, I must have been here for a couple of hours, staring at my phone and psychologically frozen. This feels time-sensitive but…come on, Nikki isn't about to actually *hurt* anybody. That's just insane. She has no reason to, anyway. I don't know everything about my assistant, but I do know that she has a penchant for melodrama. If she is actually at J's place currently and he's there, it's far more likely that J has locked her out and left her pouting than for Nikki to be a real and active threat to anyone.

Okay…okay. I need to calm down. There's no reason to freak out about this. Nikki is probably drunk or high or having some sort of mental health crisis at the very worst. She just wants to talk. I can do that. I did not want to have this heavy-ass conversation with her today, but if she's at the point where she's willing to abandon her work and send me semi-threatening text messages to get her point across, I'm willing to hear her out.

Stilling my body, I suck in a deep, deliberate breath, hold it, then let it stream out slowly between my pursed lips. My nerves are already too frazzled for this kind of foolishness. I can't afford to overreact with so much to lose.

That's why I can't call the cops. Not unless Nikki is a clear danger to herself or someone else. I could end up giving her a permanent arrest record when there's no need. I don't want to do that to her.

If this is some kind of twisted joke, though? She's definitely fired.

Good. This plan of action feels good. I'll just go to J's place – ironically the same apartment I've been avoiding so fervently – and very calmly see what's up. Nikki and I will talk, I'll gently explain to her that I can't be with her sexually anymore because she is way too emotionally unstable, and that'll be that. I'll even officially give her the rest of the week off from work to get herself together. Bonus if J is actually home and I can talk to him about our situation, too. Kill two birds with one stone.

The fact that Nikki has been silent since that last text…that's what leaves my teeth on edge and has me clenching my hands into fists over and over. I know what to do but I can't relax. This whole situation is just too crazy.

Most of the lights in the other offices are off and it's a ghost town by the time I make my way to the elevators to head outside. The hand tightly gripping the handle of my briefcase aches with the effort it takes to stop trembling. Sharp pains zip up and down my tight shoulders and upper back from all the stress I've been under. A massage will definitely be in order once I get all this behind me and get back to my life as I intended it to be.

The knots in my stomach double in size and tightness as I walk outside the building to emerge on the sidewalk, a stiff breeze ruffling the kick pleat of my skirt. When I find the rideshare already waiting when I arrive, I wave at the driver and slide into the back seat.

We greet each other and that's it; my mind is too full of turmoil to engage in my usual small talk as we drive.

Maybe I should try to call Nikki again. I release the death grip on my phone enough to quick-dial her number again, but she doesn't answer. Still doesn't when I try a few more times.

She doesn't answer any of my "hello" texts, either.

Nausea churns my stomach. My palms begin to sweat in earnest.

I close my eyes and avoid looking out of the window, knowing that the visual of drawing closer to J's place will only make me feel sicker. I force my lungs into slow drags of air in and out, in and out. Trying to calm myself down when I feel anything but.

It's fine.

Nikki's…having some kind of *moment,* but she's fine. J's fine. They're fine and so am I.

Keeping my eyes closed the entire twenty-minute ride from my job, I repeat those words in my head like a meditative mantra and just try to keep breathing.

When I get there, we're just going to talk. Because Nikki just wants to talk.

That's it – that's all we're going to do.

Nothing to be afraid of or call the cops for.

When I feel the car slow, I dare to look at my phone clutched in my lap despite knowing what I'll see – a bunch of unanswered texts. It's the silence that's making me a little crazy.

I swallow hard when the car finally rolls to a stop. The driver leaves me at the curb once I've gathered all my stuff. For a long moment, I stare up at the building that holds so many memories created in such a short time that I nearly choke on them. I'm still in my work clothes, but at least I had the presence of mind to switch out my high heels with a pair of sneakers. That makes it much easier to trudge down the long concrete path to the front doors.

As I make my way toward the elevators, I barely notice the beautiful landscaping outside or the fine furnishings in the lobby. I've always thought J's apartment building was stunning, but I can't appreciate its beauty with this hard lump of dread stuck in my throat. As it is, I feel like I'm heading toward something dark and final. Like a guillotine.

How did I get here? I feel like it's been years since J reached out to me on that app, not mere months. My life has gone through so many changes since then, I hardly recognize it anymore. I hardly recognize myself. Even Nikki, someone I have known for years, has transformed into a stranger before my eyes. A stranger with the potential to be dangerous. I've never seen this side of her before. I don't know what she's truly capable of.

But J must have. I'll never forget the icy look in his eyes the last time we talked when he warned me about Nikki. It had seemed so ridiculous at the time to be told that this diminutive woman with a killer smile could do any harm to anyone, but J had seemed convinced.

Maybe I should have listened to him. Nikki may not be capable of true violence, but she was definitely capable of causing havoc in my life.

I place one foot after the other on the fancy hallway carpet after I get off the elevator on J's floor. Each footfall feels heavier than the last the closer I come to J's apartment at the end of the hallway.

When I raise my hand to knock, the gap between the solid wood door and the frame makes me freeze. The door is open already.

I glance to my left and right only to see no one. I'm alone.

My breaths tremble as they escape my tight chest. J would never leave his door cracked like this. No way in hell. I may not know everything about him, but I know that.

The alarms in my head that I've been suppressing all day clamor back to life even as I try to stay calm and keep my breathing even and slow. "J?" Gingerly, I press forward into the apartment.

It's dark. I put both hands out to feel my way around, leaning into the wall of the hallway that leads to the spacious living room. "Nikki?" My voice breaks and sinks into the quiet, making me cringe instinctively at the grating sound. My heart is a hummingbird in my throat.

Every instinct in me is screaming for me to go in the opposite direction – for help, for my own fucking sanity. God knows I don't need any of this madness. Still, I'm a slave to that kernel of curiosity hiding in the center of my fear. I have to know what's going on.

J fed me breakfast in bed from his hand the last time I was here. It feels beyond absurd to think about that now under the circumstances, but the memory spears through my anxious thoughts and makes my heart twist in my chest. We were both naked, me still twisted up in his sheets. He'd tenderly kissed my wrists where they were raw from the rope he'd used to tie me to his bedframe. I'd sucked orange juice off his tongue. Those moments had felt like living in the center of the dreams of the future I had for myself.

That feels like a lifetime ago now.

I turn down the hall that leads to J's bedroom to see a light coming from underneath his closed door leeching into the darkness ahead of me. Darkness and more silence.

"J? Nikki?" I call for them again as I creep forward, though I probably wouldn't have heard them over my heartbeat hammering in my ears. I can barely hear myself think.

The closer I get to the bedroom door looming before me, the faster horrible scenarios start tumbling through my mind – images like one would see in a slasher movie. I have to mentally scramble to shut them down. I can't psyche myself out.

With a deep, shuddering breath, I turn the knob and push open the bedroom door.

I stumble forward a step.

J…he's there. On the bed. Lying on his back in nothing but his boxer briefs. Each wrist and ankle tied to the nearest post of the tall metal bed frame.

I stare, not breathing. I…I can't do anything else. There are stains all over the white sheets – smears of rusty brown, lines and droplets of bright red.

It looks like blood.

The part of me taking in the scene as factual information is at war with the part of me clinging to disbelief. This isn't actually happening. It can't be, but J hasn't moved at all since I opened the door. Panic washes over me, animating my body and making me surge forward. I'm too scared to speak again, afraid that if I call J's name and he doesn't answer the worst of the worst-case scenarios will have come to pass.

My hands find his face first and I press two trembling fingers to his neck, nearly collapsing with relief when I feel a pulse. But it's weak.

With all the lights on in the room, I can see everything. My eyes scan the rest of him. There are deep gouges in his wrists, deeper than mine have ever been when he and I used the rope for play. His bottom lip is split like he's been hit more than once. And he's absolutely covered in shallow cuts, although some are deeper than others. Most of them have already scabbed over but there are some – the deeper ones I discover along his back – that are fresh and actively bleeding. That's the source of the blood everywhere.

This is so much worse than I thought. This is worse than I imagined because his being knocked over the head in a burglary made more sense than this. *Nothing* about this made sense to me.

Did Nikki actually do this to him? How? J is easily three times her size and strength and she somehow managed to tie him to a bed and keep him captive for – Jesus, how long has he been here? My stomach goes ice cold. Has he literally been here since the last time I saw him weeks ago? This is why he never responded to me?

Swallowing hard, I reach for J's face and cradle it in my hands. "Hey, it's me. It's…it's Gorgeous." My heart aches as I speak aloud his nickname for me. His skin is clammy and so hot against my palms it feels like a burn. He has to be running a fever.

J's eyes remain closed and he still doesn't move. I grab his shoulders and shake him a little. "Come on, J. Wake up" I pat his cheek with a little more force. "We need to get you to a doctor." Still nothing. Shaking from head to toe, I lean in close and check to see if he's still breathing.

He is, but it's shallow. As gently as I can manage, I pull open one of his eyelids enough to see his eye and find it glassy and unfocused. He's been fucking drugged – with what, I can't tell.

A shiver of real fear courses through me and I reach for the nearest rope, the one attached to J's left wrist. The white nylon coil is thick and sturdy, twisted so many times into itself that I can't pry the knots apart with my fingers. I need some kind of knife to free him, but I don't want to leave J alone.

Sinking to my knees next to the bed, I feel like the sky is caving in around me.

God, J did not deserve this.

Nothing could have prepared me for this level of insanity. I don't think I even could have conceptualized finding J like this. What is this shit?

I also don't think I've ever felt so guilty in my life. J had tried to warn me about what my assistant was capable of and I blew him off, thinking he was being controlling and dismissive. I was accusatory and uncompromising even in the face of clear evidence that he cared about me as much as he said he did. And now…

In a consuming wave that starts at my feet, anger washes over me, sweeping away the toxic brew of guilt, confusion, fear, and concern.

Where the fuck is Nikki?

My eyes dart around the room but I see no movement save for the subtle rise and fall of J's naked chest. At least he's still breathing for now.

I need to get him free of those ropes. I yank open the drawer to his nightstand and rifle around the contents for a pocket knife or something sharp enough to cut that nylon.

"I see you made it."

Nikki's once-sweet voice is like acid in my ears now. I turn to see her slither into the room from the direction of J's closet. I've been angry enough to want to physically harm a person before, more than once. I've never wanted to squeeze the life out of someone until I look into Nikki's eyes and see a stranger that needs to be punished for hurting someone I love.

And to make matters worse, she had the audacity to be wearing the gray silk nightie I left here a while back.

"It took you long enough," Nikki says, casually even as J is splayed across his bed like a criminal on a torture rack. Rage, hot and sudden, catches me in its grip and it takes everything in me not to jump up and knock her head off. But J stirs, just a little, his fingers tightening around mine in his stupor.

It's enough to keep me still and at his side. Just barely.

"Well," I say through gritted teeth, "I'm here. What the fuck do you want?" I tighten my grip on J's fingers, trying to let him know without words that I'm here and, at this point, here only for him.

"You, Brooklyn," Nikki says simply, with a grin that stretches across her face that's cold enough to chill me to the bone.

Eleven

What had happened to my friend? Where had she gone?

I don't recognize the person I'm seeing before me.

Nikki smiles at me from where she stands across the room and I just feel outdone. I don't understand. I keep scraping the dredges of my mind for crumbs of memory, anything that could give me an inkling as to why someone I thought I was close to would do this. I can't believe she is the kind of human being that could tie someone up, leave them alone with no food or water, then *cut* them with a blade over the course of weeks. I can't. It's beyond cruel – it's sick. Sadistic for no reason.

"Nikki, did you really do this to him?" My voice is so raw and coarse with emotion it barely sounds like it belongs to me.

Nikki's fingers toy with the scalloped hem of my short nightgown, which hits her in the middle of her thighs. It was one of my favorites and now I just want to burn it to ash. She cocks her head at me, appearing to consider my words. Her eyes narrow. "He wouldn't fuck me, you know."

I blink at her in shock. *"What?"*

"I tried all my tricks," Nikki continues, slowly approaching as she stares at me. "All the shit he taught *you*, in fact. But he never gave in." Even though he's the subject of her speech, Nikki doesn't give J on the bed so much as a sideways glance, but he's all I can think about. The closer Nikki moves to me, the more I try to subtly position my body between her and J. If she did do all of this – and I'm still having a hard time believing it, even now – I have no plans to let her hurt J any more than she already has.

A hot droplet hits the back of the hand holding on to J's and startles me. I hadn't realized I was crying.

I'm tempted to throw the lamp on the nightstand at her head, but I must stay cool. She seems calm enough for now to reason with me and I need to take advantage of the opportunity. There's still a chance for all of us to get out of this. I hope.

After briefly closing my eyes, I try again. "Nikki, please. I care about you and I know you care about me. Help me…understand this. *Please.*" The Nikki I know is still in there somewhere. If she's having some kind of psychotic break, we can help her deal with that, but she needs to let me and J out of here so I don't have to get her arrested for kidnapping.

"He must love you as much as he says. As much as he told me he did." Nikki's voice sounds far away and small, almost disappointed, and her eyes are red like she's been crying. But I see no tears on her face now. "But Brooklyn, I promise he doesn't love you as much *I* do. And that's what you deserve."

Nikki smiles that smile at me again, the chilling one I've never seen before, and then her face crumples. "But you fucked me and then left me. Just like he did." She acknowledges J at last with an accusatory finger pointed his way.

"No, I didn't!" I say, and I hate the way it feels like a lie in my mouth, even though I know it isn't. "We hung out more than once since…since then." I can't hold her gaze and steal a glance at J. He's knocked out again. Shamefully, I hope he doesn't hear this part of the conversation. I'm going to tell him about Nikki and me, but I don't want him to hear about it like this. "You make it seem like I stopped talking to you."

"You were different afterward and you know it." Nikki crosses her arms over her chest, her wavy hair loose and flowing over her shoulders. She'd look beautiful if this whole situation wasn't completely fucked up.

It's clear she's not going to believe me, so I try changing the subject. "How did you even get into J's apartment?"

"He let me in."

I send her a glare. "I doubt that."

"He did when I told him I came over to talk about you. We ended up in his bedroom after a drink or two. His drink had a little something extra in it."

"So, you managed to tie him to his own bed and cut him up?" I can feel the deep scowl take over my face. The more Nikki talks, the less sense she makes.

She shrugs. Actually *shrugs*. Like this is nothing, like she hasn't committed a felony that would land her in prison for decades, like she hasn't shattered my trust and my heart into a million tiny pieces.

"I *cut* him," Nikki says, her bare feet starting to move closer to me and J once more, "so he can know the pain I feel at him taking what's mine."

"But you don't want to kill him."

"Maybe not, but I do want him to die." Her head cocks again, in the other direction this time. "You distanced yourself from me because of *him*. You treated me like shit because of *him*. It's not ideal but you'll never let him go otherwise."

My lungs seize. "You…you did this for *me?*" She was trying to keep me in a relationship with her by literally getting rid of my boyfriend? That's what this is about?

I'm going to be sick for real.

"Of course…all I want is to be together. You and me."

Shaking my head, I squeeze J's hand harder. "So, what was your plan? Just let him die here in his apartment and then you and I run off into the sunset?"

Nikki's eyes narrow once again. "Don't patronize me. I'm not a child."

"Nikki!" I huff in frustration. "*Patronize you?* This is fucking crazy! What are you talking about!?"

Before she can respond to my outburst, her lithe body shifts in the light. She has drawn close enough for me to see her in clearer detail — like the spots of dried blood all over the parts of her arms and legs that aren't covered by *my* nightgown. I guess she put it on after indulging in her depravity with J.

When Nikki takes another step forward, the glint of metal at her side catches my eye. My eyes widen. She has a kitchen knife in her hand, presumably the one she's been using on J judging by the dark smudges on the long blade.

And she's coming closer.

"I know this might be hard for you to understand," Nikki says to me as she rolls her wrist, making the knife catch the light, "but I'm doing this for us."

My mind fills to the brim with logical rebuttals as my heartbeat ramps up, but I clamp my lips shut. Nikki can't be reasoned with. I don't know if she's always been this way and our involvement pushed her over the edge, but looking back and seeing the dead look in her pretty eyes tells me the woman I thought I knew is gone. She's broken inside, and I might have been the one who did the breaking.

My face heats with shame. I should have left well enough alone, but I was only thinking about myself. Selfishness has done this to J – mine and Nikki's.

"Nikki, stop this. Please." If logic won't work to break her out of this, perhaps raw emotion could. I'm the one she says she is in love with, right? Shouldn't you want to do everything you can for the object of your affection? "None of this is necessary. Let him go, Nikki. I need to get J to a hospital, okay? No one has to die here today."

"If he doesn't, nothing changes!" Nikki's scream startles me so badly I back up a step. She reaches up with her free hand and yanks at her hair so hard it makes me wince. I'm surprised there aren't any loose strands clasped in her fist when she pulls away. "I can't be happy unless he's gone."

"That's not true, Nikki."

"Yes, it is." Nodding, she starts to pace, shifting her gaze to her feet on the rug. "Yes, it is." Her last words come out as a murmur and it sounds like she's trying to convince herself they are true. Deep down, she has to know what she's doing is wrong. Whatever this is has taken control of her mind.

Maybe she's not completely broken. I don't know if I can make a difference, but I need to at least try to get that knife out of her hand.

I don't get far in that endeavor. "Nikki – "

"Shut up."

Having never heard that tone from her before, I unintentionally do just that. "I'm happy," she says with a grim smile. "You're happy. J is going where he needs to go; you'll see."

Her words have become disjointed and strange. When she tightens her grip on the knife handle, I know we've passed the point of no return in terms of conversation. Nikki is about action right now. I have to be as well.

I need to get to my phone…but where is it?

My eyes flick from the knife in her hand to the doorway. I spot my handbag on its side just to the left of the doorway. I must have dropped it when I first came into the room and rushed to J's side.

I look back at Nikki. She's studying me instead of J, still turning the knife handle over and over in her hand. My bag is behind her. I'll have to knock her out of the way to get to it, but the thought of moving a muscle in this moment makes all my internal organs tense with fear. I still don't really know what Nikki plans to do with that knife. It might still be an empty threat. Slicing a person all over is horrible and sick, but it's still a far cry from ending their lives intentionally.

Nikki isn't a killer.

At least, I hope with everything in me she isn't. And that I can keep her at bay long enough to get some real help up here.

"You're not going to kill anybody, Nikki. Not me, not J, not yourself." I hold her gaze even though I want to look anywhere else but into the icy chill of her eyes. "Put the knife down and we can all walk out of here."

She seems to consider my words for a moment and hope bubbles up in my body. Then she considers the knife before her eyes flip up again to look at J, still unmoving on the bed. "Only two of us are leaving," she says, her voice falling quiet and lifeless and unrecognizable, and I almost don't have time to register her movement. Between one blink and the next, Nikki went from standing a few feet away to lunging for the bed with the knife in her fist, high above her head. I swear to God, if she hadn't screamed and startled me out of my dissociative haze, I wouldn't have been able to react in time.

But I did, my limbs animating without any mental command from me. My leg shoots out and kicks her back before she can bring down the knife onto J's prone form. My foot lands squarely in the middle of her narrow chest, knocking her back into a stumble a safer distance away.

"Nikki, *stop!* Are you serious – you don't have to do this!" My chest heaves with heavy breaths that feel like sandpaper in my lungs. I've ended up in some made-for-TV movie fighting for my life. God*damn…*I just had to have my cake and eat it, too – and now I'm paying for it.

Nikki, having gone down on one knee, glares at me like she can't believe I dared to stop her. As if trying to murder J in cold blood made all the sense in the world. The gleam in her eyes now is unholy. Otherworldly.

Has this – whatever this is – been lurking inside of Nikki all the years I've known her? Is this what J had seen in the past?

I had let *that* into my bed?

Nikki is breathing hard, her hair now wild from the sudden exertion of coming at us. That knife still clutched in her hand. She looks as unhinged as her behavior suggests she is. Still, I don't want to hurt her for real. I just want her to stop so I can get J out of here and get her some help.

I can't understand why she looks so shocked, her eyes wide and angry. "Why are you trying to protect him, Brooklyn?" She's screaming directly at *me* now.

"Because he hasn't done anything!" I scream back at her, the truth ringing in my words registering even as I say them. J hasn't done anything but be a human being. He made an honest mistake. He didn't deserve me taking him down with my tongue at my mom's place and he certainly didn't deserve what Nikki has done to him. I guess I was so used to him being virtually perfect, I didn't make room for grace in our relationship. That's on me. But if he and I both make it out of this situation with our lives intact, I fully intend to rectify that misstep on my part.

But that's a big "if" with Nikki being hellbent on punishing J for – for what? Existing?

I finally force myself to let go of J's hand so I can hold up both of mine in an act of surrender. I don't want to fight her. I don't want this madness to go on any longer than it already has. "Nikki, listen to me – "

"So, you were lying to me when you told me all the ways he hurt you?" Cutting me off, Nikki rises to her full height, and I step back again. Her misdirected rage has made her small stature more intimidating than I thought possible.

"No, but…" I avert my eyes. My complaints to her seem so stupid and childish now in my memory. "He didn't do any of that on purpose."

"Bullshit." The rise and fall of Nikki's chest increase in speed, like she's rallying her adrenaline for another attack, but I'm prepared to knock her on her ass again if she tries it. And as soon as she's incapacitated, I'm going for my phone and ending this.

"Nikki, *stop*. You're not thinking this through, okay? You don't want to kill anyone. Give me the knife." I stretch out my hand, palm up. Salt from the terrified tears gathers in the corners of my mouth but I ignore them. "You don't want blood on your hands. You don't want to live with the guilt of killing an innocent person. I don't know how we got here but I can tell you just want the pain to stop, and I understand that but…this isn't the way." I flex my fingers toward her in my desperation to have her listen to me. "Just *give* it to me. Please."

I see something – a flicker or a shadow – in Nikki's eyes that almost lets me believe something I've said has registered and she might actually hand over the weapon. But it's gone nearly as soon as I see it.

Nikki just grips the knife tighter, eyes wide and unblinking as she paces near the foot of J's bed a few steps at a time like a caged animal ready to die to get free. Her renewed intensity raises the hair on my arms and makes a sheen of sweat bloom over my entire body. I keep an eye on her and edge away from J's side, angling my body so that if she lunges again, I can push her hard enough to get J out of harm's way and still get to my cell in my bag on the floor.

I'm distracted when angry tears burst from her eyes and she heaves a sob. "Did you ever really love me, Brooklyn? Did you ever care that I loved you this much?"

She sounds so broken, so utterly devastated by the mere idea that I don't share her feelings that I sob too.

God, I wish I did. I wish I had been more accepting of the way J had chosen to express his love for me by surprising me with a visit to my family. I wish I had been able to give Nikki the type of relationship she clearly wanted so badly. More than anything, I wish I had been able to be honest with myself about what I wanted and needed from both of them.

The tears stream faster down my face. I turn to J, who has finally begun to stir a little, his head slowly rocking back and forth. Watching him, I'm flooded with love and affection so deep it nearly buckles my knees. I almost lost him because I insisted on acting stupid and prideful like a child instead of dealing with my feelings. I just ran away from them because I wanted to feel good and Nikki's feelings ended up being collateral damage. And that wasn't fair.

I have no idea what she had already been dealing with emotionally and psychologically before we got involved the way we did, but it's clear our situation helped push her over the edge mentally. "I'm so sorry, Nikki," I say, choking on my apology in my effort to speak around the tightness in my throat. "I know I had some part in you ending up here… like this. And I'm so sorry for that." I took a deep breath and hoped my truth wouldn't make her want to end me, too. "I do love you, but I love you as a friend."

Nikki's expression twists into something ugly. "And you love him." She jerks her chin at the bed.

It's not a question because of course she knows. I would not have thrown myself between them and risked bodily harm if I didn't. His actions would not have hurt and angered me so much otherwise. But Nikki wants confirmation. Her unknown reason for needing to hear it aloud is what makes my heart pound. Every muscle in my body tenses for action.

My eyes find J and I whimper when I see one bleary eye partially open and look up at me. The modicum of relief I feel is enough to make me lightheaded, especially considering the recent memory of the cold emptiness I felt when I let myself think of the worst happening to this man.

"I do love him," I say, barely loud enough to be heard by Nikki steps away, but definitely loud enough for J. That one eye blinks in an acknowledgment just for me.

Nikki *had* heard. I feel her energy shift once more, making me drag my gaze away from J back up to her fuming face. "You've already hurt me more than J ever did," she says, her voice trembling and way too highly pitched for her to be in a sane state of mind. "More than *anyone.*"

I watch her break in real time on that last word. See the last recognizable parts of her psyche crumble into nothing. Remorse threatens to turn me inside out as I shake with a fresh sob. I didn't mean to do this to my friend.

With a scream that sounds like it was torn from the depths of her tortured soul, Nikki lunges straight for *me* this time — at the exact moment I try to leap past her toward my bag on the floor, having expected her to go for J's neck again. The impact of our bodies knocks both of us onto our backs, leaving us gasping for air. Her elbow hit me in the stomach and sent my diaphragm into a spasm. I roll back and forth on the rug, the unexpected pain rocking my world.

Nikki and I spot the knife on the floor between us at the same time. Our eyes lock.

"Don't, Nikki." I plead with her. "Leave it!"

Nikki snatches up the knife. I'm up onto my knees in an instant, both hands clamped down on hers to keep the weapon pressed flat to the floor. She fights me, one of her long legs coming up to kick me away from her, but I expect it this time and block her with my shin. "Nikki, *stop!*"

Wrenching her hand free from mine with a cry, Nikki somehow stumbles backward and to her feet. I stare up at her from where I'm sprawled on the floor. She still managed to keep the knife in her hand.

"I can't take this anymore. Since you love him so much," Nikki whispers with tears dripping onto the front of my nightie, "you can go, too."

My mouth goes dry, throat working fruitlessly as I try to swallow.

I don't want to die today.

Nikki lifts her arm again to strike what she clearly intends to be a killing blow.

But I can't go out like that – not without a fight.

I scream and kick at her again. It's enough to make her stumble, but goddammit, she just won't go down again. And this time, I shriek as she falls away and drags the knife blade in her fist down the front of my shin, leaving a thin, red line of blood that immediately flows down my leg and drips onto J's white rug.

My leg is on fire, but I keep my eyes on Nikki to block out the searing pain.

"I guess none of us are getting out of here alive today," Nikki says, her voice grave.

"Nikki…I do love you," I say, grimacing and huffing at the pain levels rising, "but *fuck you.*"

She doesn't raise the knife this time, just runs at me for what feels like the final time.

But I don't dare look away. She'll have to look me in my eyes.

Two loud pops sound out, making me scream.

Nikki takes one heavy step forward then collapses in a heap.

I stare and stare and stare some more. Nikki's body folded at an unnatural angle when she hit the floor. She…she isn't moving.

How – I don't –

It's only then that I see the man standing in the doorway. The same man that had come looking for Nikki at the office.

He's wearing the same outfit I saw him in sans the suit jacket. Horrified, I watch him lower the pistol with which he'd just shot my friend.

"Why? *You fucking killed her!*"

The man had tears in his eyes when he spoke to me with that gravelly voice. "I had to put my wife down, ma'am. No one else could do it."

Twelve

Pop, pop.

The sound of those two gunshots plays over and over again in my mind. I can still hear them echoing in my ears.

Two rapid shots and seconds later, my friend was gone from this world, her broken body lying in a heap, her pool of blood slowly leaking out and soaking J's rug.

I can never unsee that. It's burned into my thoughts, now a permanent fixture of my psyche I'm sure will torture me in some way for the rest of my life.

After that, I'll never be the same.

"Here you go, ma'am." I glance up to see the uniformed EMT who had bandaged my leg standing over me where I sit in the back of the open ambulance in the parking lot of J's apartment complex. His crooked smile is kind when he gently places one of those thin metallic blankets over my shoulders.

I wipe at my eyes, still leaking tears that won't stop coming, and offer him a smile that is as brittle as I feel. "Thanks. For everything." Even forcing myself to project to be heard, my voice is little more than rough air. Probably from all the screaming.

"No problem. I'm glad you won't need the stitches. That was a pretty bad laceration."

When I nod and pull his offering closer around me, he nods as well and walks back to his station in the truck.

I've been out here for a while. Well, maybe. Honestly, it could have been ten minutes or ten hours — I wouldn't have been able to tell the difference. Everything has been hazy and moving at half-speed since Nikki came after me with the knife and the gunshots sounded out. My throat is dry and tight and my head feels like it's been stuffed with steel wool. I can't get my thoughts to flow in any order that makes sense. My EMT must have injected me with some good painkillers. I consider the thick white bandage wrapped around my right leg from knee to ankle, rotating my knee this way and that to see it from all angles. Despite not needing the stitches, that cut is still bound to leave a hell of a scar courtesy of my late assistant. Not too different from the one Nikki left on my life.

Movement across the parking lot draws my weary eyes. Three officers lead Nikki's supposed "husband" to one of the two police cars pulled up at the front curb of the building. His head hanging low, the man shuffles in step with the officer who has a hold on his elbow, his wrists bound in handcuffs in front of him.

"No one else could do it..." That's what he'd said to me when I screamed and demanded to know why he'd put Nikki down like a rabid fucking dog. When it was done, I'd looked into his eyes and saw he believed what he'd told me, whether it was true or not.

His suit is still clean and I can't see any cuts or bruises on his face from this distance, so it looks like he hadn't put up a fight with the cops while they were still in the building.

I never even got his name. Guess I'll never know unless I happen to catch the story of what happened today on the news.

My eyes close yet release a fresh stream of tears as a wave of grief rolls over me, heavy and cold enough to make my entire body shiver.

It didn't have to end like this. I just wanted the chance to talk to her, to get her through whatever it was she was going through, and that murderer took it away from me.

Goddammit, Nikki.

Did I ever really know her? Thinking back, she really could have had an entire second life elsewhere that I knew nothing about. She *told* me plenty of things about her family and her past, even showed me lots of photos over the years we knew each other. But thinking about it now, the photos were either of her by herself or of the people she was telling me about – never together. And I had never seen a picture or heard her talk about the man who took her life today.

He could have been telling the truth. Nikki could very well have been a menace to society and her husband was doing the Lord's work by removing her from this Earth. That doesn't make me feel any better as I watch the cop cars pull off to take him to jail for his crimes. Nikki wasn't evil; she was disturbed. And whether they were truly married or not, he didn't have the right to decide whether she lived or died.

The tightness in my throat returns when I don't manage to avert my eyes in time. Two other EMTs wheel the gurney carrying a long black bag down the sidewalk toward where the coroner's truck is parked. I'm looking at it. I was there when it happened and I still can't wrap my head around it. I still can't believe it.

Nikki is really gone. Young, beautiful…her life snuffed out as a result of her own demons. She really could have taken me with her, and J as well. The fact that she didn't brings no warmth to my heart.

No part of this horrible day isn't tragic.

I hear each door at the rear of the coroner's truck close with a heavy clank and a note of finality. Then the techs climb inside and drive away. I watch it go, steady tears streaming down my cheeks.

The truck disappears around the closest bend in the road and the sob that wracks my body would have knocked me off my feet had I been standing.

I feel like my chest is caving in. It's too much. Everything, all of it – it's way, way too much at once. I'm crying so hard I start hyperventilating and the EMT comes rushing back to my side with a handful of tissues and a warm hand on my back to keep me from falling apart.

Nikki had tried to kill me and my boyfriend.

Then Nikki was dead, murdered in front of me.

And J – *oh, God.*

What had happened to J?

I hear what sounds like a scuffle in the other ambulance that's parked a few feet away. The words are too low to make out, but the low timbre of the shouting and every cell in my body tells me the dominant voice belongs to J.

I try to stand, wobbling more than a little and having to lean against the rear of my ambulance. The EMT tries to stop me with a firm hand on my shoulder. "Ma'am, you really should sit down! Your leg – "

"I'm fine," I say, hopping down from my seat to hobble my way over to the other vehicle. Each step sends a spear of pain shooting through my leg, but I grit my teeth and ignore it. I need to see for myself that J's okay.

"J!" My entire body is hot as I yell into the back of the open ambulance for him. One tech argues with J, who is stretched out on the gurney and covered in a thin sheet from the chest down. The other sees me and hurries to help me up into the truck.

I murmur a thanks under my breath and move to stand at J's side. I look him over, losing count of the number of small bandages that cover him, even a few on his handsome face. Warm brown eyes find mine. "Hey there, Gorgeous," he says, and I lose it completely, my head dropping onto his shoulder as I cry like I'm made of tears. His closest arm has an IV in his vein, but he still raises it to gently pat my head as best he can to calm me down.

"I'm so sorry," I say, fighting the deep shudder in my body that's fueling all the tears. "This is all my fault."

"Jonathan," he says, making me squint down at him in confusion.

"What?"

"My name. You should call me that. I think we've outgrown the initials." His voice is hoarser than I've ever heard it; I have to lean down close to his face to hear. But I do, and his words light me up on the inside. Everything that happened before today feels so *stupid* now. What a waste…

His eyes grow serious as he stares into mine. "I wish I hadn't been right about Nikki. I really do. Despite all that happened, I know she was your friend."

Yeah, she was.

Still, how he manages to be so generous considering she had held him captive for weeks blows my mind. But I'm tired of thinking about it and I definitely don't want to talk about it. Any of it.

All the strength seems to bleed out of my body through my feet and I have to lean heavily against the gurney with both hands to keep myself upright.

"He's septic," the female EMT who had been arguing with him suddenly says, making me sniffle and finally raise my head. "But he's refusing to let us take him to the hospital." The tightness around her mouth suggests she strongly disagrees with that decision.

I do, too.

"J – Jonathan, you need to go to the hospital, baby. Sepsis is serious." His full name feels foreign and strange on my tongue, but its flavor is familiar. I could get used to it.

"I'll be fine," he says, bristling. J doesn't seem to want to talk about the hospital at all.

"No, you won't."

He rolls his eyes and I know he's already on the road to recovery despite all of his injuries. "Please tell these fine folks I plan on going home, right now."

That actually makes me chuckle. I'm surprised my body can even recognize the emotion of joy right now, even in such a small measure.

"Listen, *Jonathan,*" I say, leaning closer to him, "I'll make you a deal. We go to the hospital now, then you come home with me when you get out and I'll take care of you. Plus," I continue, already sobering, "we still have a lot to talk about."

Jonathan swallows hard then gives me a nod of agreement, squeezing my hand as the male EMT closes the doors and we head off to the hospital.

But there's still much more healing to do besides the physical. For both of us.

One Year Later

It's theme night again at the BDSM club. I've never been more excited than I am tonight.

Bacchanal; that's the theme. Beauty, excess, indulgence and joy. All the things I see as I stare at my husband below me on the bed. Black silk sheets glide over our skin, totally bare to each other save for the short black masks that cover just our eyes.

J – these days I only call him Jonathan when I'm upset with him – groans louder with every roll of my hips, but I can hardly hear him for the roar of the packed house all around us, cheering us on. We're the main event tonight and I can feel their erotic energy feeding my own.

But J and I only have eyes for each other. I ride him slow then fast, churning my hips then bucking hard. His hands don't paw at my ass – instead, one is on the back of my neck, his fingers reaching into my curls to pull my head down toward him. The other is at my jaw, gentle and perfect. Our wedding rings catch the light; just seeing them makes me hum with pleasure, even as my fingers stroke over the thin, straight scars Nikki left behind. I have them, too, but mine are much deeper. And they are just as easy for J to see.

After everything that happened, J ended up in the hospital for three days, pumped full of antibiotics for the infection and saline solution for the dehydration. I took off from work for the first time in years to stay with him, feeding him soup by the spoonful and heeding to his every beck and call. When he was discharged, I took him home with me and we laid all our cards on the table – families, friends, hopes, dreams…our pasts and our expectations for the future. I didn't want to leave anything to chance or open to interpretation ever again. When I think about how much I lost, of how much I *could* have lost…it was too much to bear.

True to his word, J introduced me to his parents and older brother within a couple of weeks of our conversation. Before I knew it, we had moved in together and J was coming to dinner at my mom's house every week like he had been doing it all along. This time, we made that decision together, and that made all the difference in the world.

Right now, we're fucking for our audience like it's the last time, though we know we'll do this for the rest of our lives, as long as we are able. I'm not ashamed – not of my desires, not of how our story began. Not anymore. J finally lays gentle hands on my breasts, swollen and tender with the early pregnancy we haven't yet announced. For now, it's our little secret. Just like our…colorful sex life. Not because it's bad or shameful, but because it's just for us.

I know he's close when I see the whites of his eyes from them rolling back in his head. I am, too, my pregnancy making everything extra sensitive.

So, I lean forward, my lips to J's hear, and whisper that I love him more than anything – our ritual. He turns his head so he can whisper back that he loves me more than life.

And as we manage to launch ourselves into heaven simultaneously, I believe it with all my being.

About the Author

Brooke Dean is a mother, storyteller, content creator, producer, author, and Director of Production Operations with over 20 years of television and digital media experience having worked at MSNBC, A+E Television Networks and Audible, Inc. A native Philadelphian now a New York City transplant, Brooke currently resides in Queens with her son Jaxon, who is also the author of the children's book series *The Whisker Gang*.

www.brookeddean.com

IG @brookedeanauthor

9 781962 870184